TEMPTED BY
HELL
ERIN BEDFORD

Tempted By Hell © 2018 Embrace the
Fantasy Publishing, LLC

Also by Erin Bedford

The Underground Series
Chasing Rabbits
Chasing Cats
Chasing Princes
Chasing Shadows
Chasing Hearts
The Crimes of Alice

The Mary Wiles Chronicles
Marked by Hell
Bound by Hell
Deceived by Hell
Tempted by Hell

Starcrossed Dragons
Riding Lightning
Grinding Frost
Swallowing Fire
Pounding Earth

The Celestial War Chronicles
Song of Blood and Fire

Crimson Fold
Until Midnight
Until Dawn
Until Sunset
Until Twilight

TEMPTED BY
HELL

ERIN BEDFORD

BONES CRUNCHED UNDER MY hand as I pounded my fist into the face of the woman before me, but she only threw her head back and laughed. Gritting my teeth, I shoved my dark hair out of my face and winced, my fingers sensitive after so much abuse. My hand tightened around the butt of my Glock 42, and my trigger finger itched to end the useless mess before me.

Tied to a chair, the demon-possessed woman watched me with growing amusement. Her laughter was unsettling. I was the one who had her by the short hairs, but she acted like I was less than the roaches crawling around on the floor of the abandoned building I'd taken her too.

The woman the demon had decided to house up in was a pretty, petite thing. Blonde hair that curled around her ears and an upturned nose that no doubt stayed even higher than that in the air. I hadn't meant to take her here. I'd been out patrolling as usual. Looking for some way into Hell. Some way to get Sid back.

"Tell me where it is," I growled, shoving my face into the woman's personal space. Her aura stank of the black inkiness of the demon writhing around inside of her. The woman's soul wasn't even a blip on the radar. Not that I cared much about that now. I was too far gone to care about casualties.

Months. It had been months since Sid had been taken and I was still no closer to finding him. So, it was only natural I'd be a bit on edge.

The demon spat blood at me, making me flinch as it hit my face. I wiped my hand over my eyes and then, without warning, whipped the gun around and slammed it across her head. The demon howled, but then her cries turned to a hacking laugh.

"You know what's funny?" the demon hissed through the pretty secretary's bow-shaped mouth. "How far the great archangel Muriel has fallen in her quest for vengeance. It's just so..." She grinned maliciously at me, obscenely licking her lips. "... delicious."

I didn't answer her taunts. A white buzzing in my head had kept me from feeling the guilt she was obviously trying to inflict on me. Angels weren't supposed to hurt humans, possessed or not. However, I wasn't particularly fond of Heaven right now. Not since I found out that they had been keeping secrets from me. Like how my leader and hero, Ramiel, had fallen all on his own, and they simply let me go after him. Had let me get captured by demons.

Fuck them.

I slammed my fist into the woman's gut with a sinister smile this time. "You're not doing yourself any favors right now. Why don't you make this easy for both of us and tell me what I want to know?" I gripped the sides of the chair, my fingernails digging into the arms of her long-sleeved silk shirt. It had started out a pale pink but had long turned to a muddy brown. Violence had a way of taking something pure and beautiful and turning into something unrecognizable. Ripping away all that was good about it until all that was left was shit.

The demon chortled, its voice gravel in the woman's throat. "Why don't you ask your boyfriend? Oh, right. You can't." The demon only had a second to cackle before I put the barrel of my gun to its head and pulled the trigger. The demon screeched but was cut off as the holy bullet ripped through the woman's skull and tore into the demon's essence. If it had been cooperative, I'd have exorcized it, and it would have gotten to go back to Hell. Sure, it'd have to claw its way back into this world, but it beat being destroyed completely.

The shot I'd fired had echoed through the building, but I wasn't worried about being heard. In this neighborhood, one more gunshot was just another Wednesday. However, the body of the deceased secretary was a problem.

Sighing in frustration, I glared at the dead woman before me. I hadn't planned on killing her. When I first caught the demon, I could feel the soul trapped inside of the secretary. I could have easily cast the demon out and saved her. However, this demon was one of

Asmodeus' followers. It'd been one of the first ones I'd come across since the demon lord had disappeared into Hell along with his son - my so-called boyfriend - Sid. Michael's dagger had also made the trip to Hell with them. The only known object to be able to rip the fabric of time and space to open a portal to Hell, and as I'd recently been informed, Heaven.

However, because of my short temper, I had destroyed the only clue I had to finding my way to back into Hell. Earlier this year I wouldn't have been itching to get back into that dank hole where I'd been tortured for God only knew for how long before I'd been miraculously freed sans my wings. Even now a part of me shuddered at the thought of going back, but we all did things we didn't want to do for the sake of the ones we loved. Whether we've admitted the emotion or not.

Tucking my gun back in its holster, I went about cleaning up the abandoned house I had used to interrogate the demon. There wasn't much to clean up, to be honest. It'd been some crack den or drug dealer's hideout. It already had questionable stains coloring the hardwood floor. What was one more?

Over the last few weeks, I'd gotten pretty good at cleaning up after myself. I didn't need the Los Angeles Police Department finding my DNA on the crime scenes. Not that it would do them any good. All my documents were forged, and I'd been very careful not to leave any trace of DNA in my time on Earth. Besides the occasional trip to the hospital but then again, the one doctor who had become too interested in the peculiar properties in my angelic blood had almost died trying to use it on himself.

Forensic evidence aside, I doubted Sergeant Thompson would slap cuffs on me any time soon, not after the demon showdown he and his fellow officers had helped me deal with. Still, better safe than sorry. I had one or two law officers who didn't particularly like me.

After making sure I was clear, I pulled my phone out and pressed my speed dial.

"Los Angeles Police Department, what's your emergency?" a pleasant female voice came over the line.

Not bothering to change my voice or disguise myself, they couldn't tell anyway, I said, "I have a dead body in a rundown

12

house on the corner of Vermont and Manchester."

"Ma'am if you could give me your name—
"

I pressed the end button. They wouldn't be able to call me back. Trisha, my favorite secretary and resident tech genius, had made sure of that. Sometimes I didn't know what I'd do without that girl, except when she was heckling me like a mother hen.

Rubbing the back of my neck, I started down the street. The sky was dark and the street empty. At least, this part of town was rundown enough not to have to worry about traffic cameras catching me leaving. I'd be surprised if anyone found anything that would point back to me. If they did, Sergeant Thompson would quickly explain it away.

Sid's black 4x4 truck sat on the lonely street, the only eye-catching object on the road announcing my presence. Soon, even that would be gone. I probably shouldn't have used it since the man in question was missing, but it seemed silly to let it go to waste when I had to do late night runs like this. Plus, Trisha's mother would kill me if I let her drive me around to hunt demons.

13

Hopping up into the driver seat, I cranked the engine and pulled onto the road, not letting myself think about the dead end I'd found myself in again. How I had failed Sid again.

The first few days after I had used my holy powers in our fight against Asmodeus had been bad. Not 'I have a hangover' bad, but 'the world has collapsed on top of me, and we were all going to hell' bad. Luckily, I had Trisha and my other best friend, Adara, there to help me through.

They had taken turns holding my hand and sneaking me in something other than hospital food. By the time I was out of the hospital, I was seething with desperation. I couldn't even imagine the things going on there. Sid was half demon, so maybe it was easier for him? Maybe he didn't find the darkness so debilitating? With the way things had been left with his father, I didn't see him being welcomed like the prince of Hell he could have been.

Pulling up to my office building, I turned the truck off and just sat. The office of Mary Wiles Private Investigation sat on top of what used to be a magic shop owned by Madame Serena. However, even my neighbors weren't safe from my job. Asmodeus had Ramiel kill the sweet but strange psychic to send a message to me. Now, the whole building belonged to me. In a way, Madame Serena was still looking out for me.

Finally getting out of the truck, I trudged toward the door between the old magic shop and Lou's. The smell of Chinese food made my stomach rumble, but the stench of demon on my body kept me from entering the shop. Shower first, then food.

I pounded up the stairs to the only door at the top. The frosted glass window had my name and business on it but also doubled as my home. Unlocking the door, I pushed it open without a care, unstrapping my gun holster as I kicked my boots off.

I stripped my clothes off as I walked through the reception area that housed a ratty couch and Trisha's desk. I barely glanced at Trisha's desk as I made my way to my room. It was well past nine, she'd be gone for the day, or she better be. I did not want another visit from her mother. Though, over eighteen Trisha still lived with her parents and worked for me because she got a bit too cocky about her hacking abilities.

Let's just say the government does not have a sense of humor.

Her mother had made the mistake of thinking that working at a desk job would keep Trisha safe and out of trouble. Boy, was she wrong. I could still remember the sting of her hand hitting my face.

For a prissy lady, she sure could hit.

Shaking my head at my thoughts, I walked through the second door that housed my office. I didn't think much of the light already on, Trisha tended to leave it on after an incident where I'd left my bloody demon-stinking clothes in a pile in front of the door. One tripping accident, a black eye, and my electric bill went up.

I'd already completely stripped by the time I got through the door and had my mind firmly set on a shower. I had to wash the demon gunk from my body and aura before it made me sick.

However, I barely made it a few feet into the room before a throat cleared, making me jerk to a stop.

Slowly, I turned to see not only Trisha sitting behind my desk but a couple in their mid-fifties gaping in my client chairs. Trisha wore a black short-sleeved shirt with a long-sleeved purple and black striped shirt beneath. Her blonde hair dyed ebony was a touch darker than my own naturally colored hair. She had also added long strips of pink and purple that matched her heavily made-up eyes. When I met those eyes, they widened a fraction letting me know how awkward I was making her feel right now. I wished I could say it was a rare occurrence for us but though, I looked like a human, ate, slept, and shit like one, I sometimes forgot to act like one. Modesty being the major one. One that the couple before me clearly appreciated.

The way they were dressed, the older couple could have come straight from Sunday mass. A large pastel pink hat sat on the woman's head her brown eyes wide with horror at my appearance. Her husband - I assumed by the wedding rings – wore a gray suit with a pale pink tie to match his wife's skirt suit. His eyes roamed over my bare skin, obviously enjoying the view.

"Uh, Mary, this is Mister and Misses Barnes. They want you to help them find their son." Trisha gave a bright smile that cracked at the edges as she gestured toward the couple.

My eyebrows shot to my hairline, and before I could think better of it, I stepped forward and held my hand out. "Mary Wiles, I apologize for my state of undress, but we usually don't have clients this late." I shot Trisha a warning look which she promptly ignored.

The husband shifted out of his seat and started to take my hand, but his wife grabbed hold of the back of his jacket and jerked him back into his seat, smacking him on the shoulder and a glower.

Trisha chuckled nervously and shifted in her, I mean, my seat.

Humans and their thing about skin. It was merely flesh. I would never understand their need to be embarrassed by their own bodies.

"Mary, why don't you go clean up and then we can talk? After all, the Barneses did come all the way from Nevada to see you, hence the late hour." The tone of Trisha's voice told me it was not a suggestion.

When exactly did she become the boss? Also, I didn't remember telling her she could accept clients for me. We'd have to discuss that later, when we didn't have a potentially paying audience.

Giving her a sharp nod, I offered the couple another smile before heading to the bathroom. On my way there, I could hear the wife muttering to her husband, "Did you see that blood on her?"

Her husband stupidly followed her question with, "Did you see that rack?"

His question resulted in a thud which I could only assume had come from his wife. If Trisha was hitting clients, we had another issue altogether.

Sighing, I turned the water on and hopped into the shower. The water washed away the grime and blood as well as the demon aura clinging to me. The moment we had moved in, I'd dropped a holy cross into the water tank. When you were constantly dealing with demons, having a priest bless and detox you became pricey. The one-time blessing on a cross was so much easier.

You'd think that being an angel, I could bless things on my own. Pfft. Not so much. Nowadays, I was lucky to exorcize a demon, let alone bless anyone. Especially not since I used my holy powers on Asmodeus. Fat lot of good that did. I would have taken him out if Ramiel hadn't jumped in front of him. Just thinking about it made my blood boil.

The shower curtain pulled back. I jumped in place, my hand grabbing for the knife I kept tucked in the shower rack. When I saw Trisha, I shoved the knife back in its place with a growl.

"Geez, jumpy much." Trisha frowned at me, her arms crossed over her chest. She had chosen to wear jeans today instead of one of her impractical flouncy skirts with its many petticoats. I'd told her more than once it would have a hand in her death one day. I only hoped I wouldn't be the leading cause of it.

Giving her a tired eye roll, I focused on scrubbing my body clean. "I have reason to be, don't you think?"

Trisha let out an exasperated sigh. "About that. We need to talk."

Suddenly, I realized that the office was quiet. "Why aren't you out there with the clients? The clients you scheduled out of work hours without consulting me?" I couldn't seem to help the irritation that filled my voice. I wasn't even that mad about it, but for some reason, I was still lashing out at her.

Placing a hand on her hip and cocking it to the side, Trisha stared me down. "First off, I sent them to their hotel. They'll come back tomorrow." She held up a finger when I started to open my mouth. "You're welcome. Secondly, someone here has to worry about keeping the lights on in this place, and that sure as hell isn't going to be you."

"What's that supposed to mean?" I turned the water off and stepped out of the shower, forcing Trisha to move back as I grabbed a towel.

"You might own the whole building thanks to Madame Serena," - she gestured around the area with her arms - "but it still requires utilities, water, gas, and last time I checked, you still have to eat. You're not going to get that from hunting down demons like you're possessed."

"I'm not possessed," I insisted, drying my hair with the towel and heading into the office. "I'm just highly motivated."

Trisha grabbed my hand, stopping me. Her shoulders sagged as she frowned. "And I get that. I do. I want to get Sid back as much as you do, but you can't let the rest of your life go to shit because of it. Life goes on, and until Adara gets back to us with some other way to get into Hell, then you're SOL."

"Sol?" I arched a brow at her.

"Shit out of luck."

Not commenting on her human slang, I pulled on a pair of sweats and a t-shirt before heading to the mini fridge. Frowning at the lack of food, my stomach rumbled in protest. Seemed my little secretary was right about some things.

"So," Trisha said as she hopped up onto the desk while I pulled the fold-up bed out of the couch sitting opposite of the room, "tell me that your almost-losing-us-a-client-because-of-your-lack-of-social-decency was the result of a good hunt?"

"I wasn't hunting," I answered immediately, even though I felt the lie on my tongue. I sat down on the bed and frowned. Why had I lied? It seemed the longer on Earth I stayed, the more human I became. Things like lying were not things I had ever thought were important. Now, it slipped out as easily as breathing.

Trisha didn't bother correcting me but came over to sit beside me on the bed. "Mary." The tone of her voice was the kind you would use for someone injured or a small child, not for an angel of God. It annoyed me for some unknown reason.

"I'm fine."

"No, you're not." Trisha didn't respond to the snap in my voice. "You're hurting. It's only natural to lash out at those around you. To feel like you have to do something because you feel powerless just sitting still. It's human."

"I'm not human," I reminded her. My fingers curled into fists and glared down at my lap.

Placing a hand on my shoulder, Trisha patted it. "I'll go grab some Chinese and then we're going to watch a crappy movie and pretend like everything is fine."

"Why?" I asked while she stood from the bed. "Why pretend?"

Trisha gave me a sad smile. "Because it's human."

2

THE SMELL OF COFFEE wafted through the office. My head jerked up from where it had landed last night, in a pile of napkins and sauce packets from Lou's. Groaning, I rubbed my eyes and inched up, the paper bags wrinkling underneath my body as I moved.

Blinking into the room, I searched for Trisha, the only one who would have made coffee already. Blessed coffee. I'd never thought I'd be addicted to anything in this world, but caffeine had quickly become my drug of choice. I blamed Trisha for that. She'd introduced me to the hellish liquid and fed my need. However, her corruptive multicolored head was nowhere to be found. Putting her absence aside, I threw my legs over the bed and hung my head between my arms.

Last night had been harder than expected. Our 'eat Chinese and watch crappy movies' plan ended up with Trisha pulling a bottle of vodka out of nowhere. I remembered the burning in my throat and a feeling of lightness and then nothing.

My head pounded, and my mouth felt as if I had swallowed a bag of cotton balls. I was no doubt suffering from massive dehydration. I could feel the cells in my body constricting, and my skin pulled tight from lack of moisture. I didn't understand why humans would subject themselves to this kind of torture.

"Good morning, sunshine!" Trisha's overly chipper voice pierced my ears like someone had shoved a hot poker into my eardrums.

I winced and flinched away from the sound. The bed dipped beside me, and a cold pressure touched my arm. I turned slightly to see a bottle of water being handed to me. Taking the bottle, I twisted the cap and poured hefty amounts into my mouth. The cool liquid coated my throat and quenched my thirst. The pounding in my head lessened slightly, but I still felt like utter garbage.

"Here." Trisha shoved a hand at me, giving me two tablets. I cocked a brow at her. Even that hurt. How was that possible? Trisha pushed my hand closer to me. "Come on, it'll help."

Sighing in defeat, I took the tablets and shoved them into my mouth, using the water to wash them down. I expected them to work instantly, but of course, they didn't. Hanging my head once more, I muttered, "What the hell happened last night?"

Trisha giggled, the sound that didn't use to bother me suddenly the most annoying sound in the world. "Well, it's quite obvious. You got drunk, and now you're hung over."

I shook my head and instantly regretted it, my eyes wobbling in my head. "I can't get drunk." My metabolism was a lot faster than an average human, making things like drugs and alcohol process through my body faster. Sid and Trisha had tried many times. Even Adara. They got a kick out of seeing how it would affect me. However, none of them had ever prevailed. The fact that caffeine even did anything was nothing short of a miracle, though I had to drink copious quantities of coffee for it to have an effect.

The bed shifted beside me again, and Trisha stood. "Tell that to the massive hangover you have now." She smacked me on the back, and I grunted. "You might feel like shit now, but trust me, you needed it."

I finally glanced up completely and watched her flounce across the room to the coffee pot. She had her hair in pigtails high up on her head today. Hot pink and teal locks mixed with the black strands of her hair, matching the teal colored corset top and shiny leather pants. Her combat boots had hot pink laces and made a loud thudding noise as they hit the ground.

"Could you walk quieter?" I watched as she poured a cup of coffee, and even that sound reverberated off the walls like a blaring horn.

Snorting, Trisha turned back to me. "It'll pass. Give the medicine a chance to work." Crossing the room, she handed me the coffee. "Here, drink up. The Barneses will be back here in an hour or so. We don't need to add alcoholic to nudist." She grinned at me cheekily.

I swallowed a few mouthfuls of the coffee, the caffeine surprisingly helping with the headache. "So, what happened last night?"

Trisha shrugged and flopped back down on the bed. "We ate Chinese, watched some bad romances, and you got totally wasted." She chuckled slightly and then, at my frown, sighed. "Look, don't beat yourself up about. You needed it. This thing with Sid? It's killing all of us. Sometimes you need to let loose, have a good cry, and let it all out there."

"I cried?"

Giving me a soft look, Trisha nodded. "Like a baby. Now drink up and then hit the shower. You smell like fortune cookies and vodka." She leaned over and gave me a whiff before grimacing. "Not an appealing smell."

Rolling my eyes, I finished my cup of coffee and shoved it back at her. Standing, I started to disrobe, but Trisha made a sound. Stopping in mid-lift of my shirt, I turned to her. "What?"

Crossing one leg over the other, Trisha leveled a stare at me. "New rule. Clothes should remain on at all times unless in the bathroom or during sexy time. Got it?"

I puffed out a breath of air. "Fine, but no more clients after hours. I can't hunt demons and pretend to be human at the same time. It's exhausting."

"I can imagine." Trisha inclined her head and then hit my leg with her boot. "Now get going. We don't want another scene, do we? I'd hate to lose the one client we have."

My lips twisted into a grimace. If I had it my way, we wouldn't have any clients. It would only be the demons and me. Then at least, maybe I would get some answers. As it stood, I wasn't any closer to getting into Hell or getting Sid back. Based on the effects the alcohol had on me, my angelic abilities were quickly failing me, giving me an even tighter deadline than before. If I thought my chances of saving Sid had been slim before, it would be impossible to save him as a regular old human. My life expectancy would definitely shorten.

While Trisha did whatever she did to prepare for clients, I washed thoroughly. The pounding in my head slowly inched to an ebbing, and though not completely gone, it was a lot more manageable. Becoming human had never been in the job description. I also never expected to be stuck on Earth this long. Sometimes I wish I'd stayed in Hell.

Flashing of blood and the sound of screams filled my mind, making me grimace. Okay, maybe not. Endless torture and mind-numbing darkness, not exactly something one fantasies about. Not anyone sane anyway.

I sighed heavily and turned off the water. Throwing the curtain back, I grabbed a towel. Quickly drying off, I caught a glimpse of myself in the mirror. Wet black hair clung to my shoulders, my pale skin even paler after last night's events. There were bags under my eyes, and the color of my irises had dulled considerably as if all the life in my had been sucked out and all that was left was an empty shell.

Not far off actually.

Ever since Sid had been taken, I'd been... off. It was strange. I was an angel of the Lord. The only thing that should affect me was the groundbreaking, earth-shattering end of the world apocalypse, not my boyfriend getting kidnapped by a demon lord.

I was acting like one of those sad pathetic women in Trisha's movies. Someone whose entire life, their very being, revolved around a single person, their guy.

And yet. And yet.

And yet my heart was breaking into a thousand pieces and it would only get worse until I had Sid before me once more. Or died trying.

A banging on the door made my eyes jerk away from the mirror. "Hurry up in there. The Barneses are here." Trisha banged on the door one more time for good measure before it was quiet again.

Taking a deep breath, I turned my eyes to the heavens, or rather the ceiling. What am I doing here, God? Why haven't you taken me back into Your embrace? Have I not been a faithful servant? Sure, there was one bout of rebellion, but that was really just me taking the initiative. Could I really be punished for that?

When I got no response, I shook my head. I didn't know why I bothered. God hadn't listened to my pleas before, why would He now?

After I pulled on a pair of jeans and a dark blue V-neck shirt, I opened the bathroom door. My bare feet touched the cool office floor, and a shiver ran through me. I searched the office for my boots. They weren't where I left them last, nor were they by the bed or the door.

I started toward the door intending to look in the waiting area but then caught sight of one boot peeking out from underneath the desk. Moving around the desk, I knelt on the ground and reached for my shoes. The moment my hand wrapped around the shoe, the office door opened.

"Trust me, Mary isn't like what you saw last night. Last night was a fluke. A job gone bad. Rarely, rarely ever happens. Promise," Trisha's voice reassured whoever had come in with her.

"Well, I sure hope so." Mrs. Barnes sniffed. "We had such high hopes for Ms. Wiles to help find our Henry. She's our last hope in finding him." She made a rude noise. "And after last night, I'm beginning to feel like we made a mistake in coming here."

"You didn't—" Trisha tried to step in, but Mrs. Barnes cut her off.

"So far it seems all we did by coming down here was give my husband a free peep show by that slut you call a detective."

My head jerked up, and it banged on the bottom of the desk. Pain laced through me as I rubbed it and shifted out from beneath. My eyes went up to the staring gaze of Trisha and the Barneses.

"I was looking for my shoes." I felt the need to explain at their questioning gaze. Then I turned my eyes to Mrs. Barnes. "And I am hardly what you would call a slut. I've only had sex once, though I am quite eager to do it again."

Mrs. Barnes gasped as her husband chuckled and leered at me.

"That's it, we're leaving." Mrs. Barnes grabbed her husband's arm and tried to drag him out of the room as Trisha jumped in front of her.

"Hold on just a moment. That's not what Mary meant. She's talking about her boyfriend. She's not hitting on your husband." Trisha shot me a glare. "While Mary might be a bit socially inept, she is really good at her job and like you said your only chance at finding your son."

Mrs. Barnes didn't seem moved by Trisha's explanation. However, Mr. Barnes was more than willing to listen. Whether it be because of Trisha's words or because he hoped I'd do something else out of the norm, I couldn't tell.

"Come now, Melissa." He touched her on the arm and gave her a soft look. "We can't find Henry without them. Don't you want to get our boy back?"

Mrs. Barnes frowned and stared down at the ground for a moment. Then she sighed and met her husband's smile with one of her own. She turned her gaze on me, and that smile fell flat.

"Understand this, I might need your help but don't think that will stop me from dropping you the moment you look the wrong way at my husband." She pointed a finger at me, the warning in her face and tone clear.

Holding my hands up which still had my boot in it, I smiled tightly back at her. "Not a problem."

Trisha led the couple to the pair of chairs before my desk while I finished putting my boots on. She sat a fresh mug of coffee on my desk before me and then turned to the couple. "Coffee, anyone?"

"No." Mrs. Barnes sniffed. "I want to get this over with."

"I'll have some." Mr. Barnes held up a finger and smiled politely at Trisha as his wife glared at him.

Clearing my throat, I pulled their attention back to me. I leaned forward in my seat, lacing my hands together in front of me on the desk. "Why don't you tell me what happened to your son and why you believe I'm the only one who can help him?"

"Our son's name is Henry." Mrs. Barnes shifted in her seat, pulling her purse into her lap. Today she wore a floral blouse of pink and purple, her skirt a darker plum shade. The bag could only be considered a bag because purse seemed an ill-equipped word for the monstrosity that covered her whole lap. I could fit a small arsenal in that bag and still have room for a few tacos. However, I didn't think Mrs. Barnes was the type to keep food on-hand like that.

"Do you have a picture of him?" I barely had time to ask before she pulled a rectangular image out of her bag. She held it out in front of her as if she expected me to get up and take it.

Thankfully, Trisha came back over with Mr. Barnes's coffee and took the picture. She handed it to me after she gave Mr. Barnes his cup. Coming around the desk, she stood at my right shoulder looking down on the image with me.

Henry Barnes was an attractive young man. He couldn't be much older than twenty with brown hair and a dusting of freckles across the bridge of his nose. I could see the similarities in him and his parents. He had his mother's eyes and his father's nose. He wore his hair shaggy, so it brushed over his forehead and hid his ears. The lopsided grin on his lips could only be described as mischievous.

"He's very handsome." Trisha glanced up from the picture to the couple before us. "How old is he?"

"Nineteen," Mr. Barnes answered as Mrs. Barnes said, "Too good for you."

Geez. Someone needed a deep cleansing of their soul. I didn't even need to use my powers to see the muddled mess that was this woman's soul.

Trisha took her comment in stride though. "What was Henry doing before he disappeared? Was he in school? Working?"

"Henry goes to the Nevada State College," Mr. Barnes told us with a proud puff of his chest.

"He was studying Pre-Law," Mrs. Barnes added.

"Art History with a Pre-Law concentration," Mr. Barnes corrected his wife, earning him a glower. It seemed someone didn't like their son's choice in careers.

Mrs. Barnes clutched her bag tightly in her hands and turned that laser gaze my way. "Henry is a bright boy, but he did have his flighty moments. This Art History thing for one. Who actually ever uses something like that?" She scoffed and shook her head. "If he had simply focused on his law degree, none of this would have happened."

"Why do you say that?" I glanced at Trisha who seemed as intrigued as I was.

Mrs. Barnes started to answer but her husband cut in. "Henry had some friends in the art community that were not exactly what you would call stand up citizens."

"Partying all night and sleeping all day." Mrs. Barnes shook her head with clear disgust on her face. "Ever since Henry started to spend more time with them, he's been missing classes, forgetting to call home, and now he's gone missing altogether."

"And you've reported this all to the police?"

Mrs. Barnes growled angrily. "Of course, I have. You think they would listen? They think he's just another college kid getting caught up in the party life and we're his overbearing parents."

I couldn't exactly argue the Nevada police's reasoning. It sounded exactly like what she had described.

"So, why do you think I can help? There's plenty of P.I.s where you live." I tapped my fingers on the desk, my brows drawn together.

"Because..." Mrs. Barnes shifted uncomfortably in her seat her eyes not meeting mine. "We've asked around about these so-called people, and they're... they're not right. There's something wrong with them."

"How so?" Trisha asked, leaning against the side of the desk.

"For starters, Henry is not the first one to go missing after hanging around these people," Mr. Barnes explained, pulling a piece of paper from his pocket. He handed it over to Trisha who glanced at it then handed it to me.

Nine names were listed with dates and ages. One or two would be nothing out of the ordinary. Even four would be a coincidence but this many? That spelled trouble with a capital Hell.

Smoothing the paper on the desktop, I met the Barnes' gaze. "Alright, I'll take the case, but it's not going to be cheap. I'll have to close up shop here while I'm in Nevada which will take time."

"Anything," Mrs. Barnes eagerly breathed, her previous dislike of me having been forgotten.

Mr. Barnes took his wife's hand and settled me with a serious dip of his chin. "Money is no issue."

I could see Trisha's barely contained excitement next to me at his words. If we were in one of her cartoons, she'd have money symbols in her eyes and her heart would be jumping out of her chest. I placed my hand closer to her hip as a reminder for her to chill out.

"I think I have all the information I need for now. I will contact the local police and find out what they already know before starting my own investigation." I stood from my seat indicating they should as well.

"When can you come to Nevada? When can you find my son?" Mrs. Barnes moved toward me as I circled the desk. Mr. Barnes wrapped an arm around her waist drawing the distraught woman closer to him.

"I have to finish up a few things here, but I will come as soon as I can. Trisha can help you with the paperwork as well as my retainer fee. I will call you as soon as I find anything out." I offered them a reassuring smile, but I didn't think it helped much.

Trisha led Mrs. Barnes to the waiting area, but Mr. Barnes hung back. I watched him curiously. What now?

"I didn't want to say this in front of my wife, but there's a club that Henry used to frequent. I was able to pull up his bank records. His account is still linked to ours."

"Oh?"

"Banquet de Rouge. If anyone knows anything, I'm sure it will be there."

"Thank you, Mr. Barnes. I'm sure it will help." I nodded as he left and then frowned. Banquet de Rouge. Feast of Red. Fucking vampires. And here I thought it would be a simple search-and-retrieve case.

"Thank you once more for choosing Wiles Investigations." Trisha beamed at the Barneses as they walked out the office door. Closing the door behind them, she sagged against it. "Well, that's over and done with."

I shot her a withering glare. The Barneses were as big of a pain in the ass today as they were last night. Even more so that now that I had to grin and bear it, be all customer services and crap. I couldn't even use the excuse that it wasn't my kind of case. Fucking vampires.

"I don't like this," I complained, sitting on the edge of her desk. "We don't have time for this. We should be working on a way to get to Hell, not finding some annoying woman's son."

Trisha rolled her eyes. "Well, that's not going very well is it?" She bumped me on the

41

shoulder as she went to her chair. Shaking the mouse to wake up her computer, she typed away on the keyboard. "So, I figured we'd check all the missing persons reports. See what the local police had on file before we start our part of the investigation. Could you give Thompson a call? Or better yet go by there? He has left a few messages about needing to talk."

"No need for that. It's vampires."

Trisha stopped typing and gaped at me. "You mean like blood sucking, night of the living dead vampires?"

"Yeah." Sighing, I dragged a hand through my half-dried hair. "Mr. Barnes pretty much confirmed it while you were getting payment. Which after all this trouble I hope you got?"

Grinning like a fiend, Trisha held up a check. "Got it. So, should we call Adara? Vampires are her area of expertise, right?"

I snorted. "If we wanted to screw them to death. In any case, I need her here finding us a way into Hell. A few vampires I can deal with."

"Okay, so then we do it the right way. Meaning you need to go see Thompson." She pointed a finger at me with a knowing look.

"I would rather not. He's just going to want my help on some case I don't have time for. I already don't—"

"Have time for any of this. Yeah, yeah." Trisha waved a hand over her shoulder, resuming her typing. "You're a regular broken record."

"A what?" My brows furrowed together tightly.

Trisha paused in her typing and glanced up at me. "You know, a record. That you play music on." When I still only stared at her, she shook her head. "You know what, forget it." Shoving her chair back, she crossed her arms over her chest and tapped her foot. "Look, I get where you are coming from, but until we find something concrete, we still have a job to do, and sadly that requires help from the local police force sometimes. And if they happen to want help in return, well..." She cocked her head to the side and gave me a wry grin. "You scratch their back, they—"

"I got it." I put my hand up to stop her and then let out a heavy breath. "Fine. I'll go

43

make nice with the police." I grimaced and shuddered. "I hate that place. There's just so much... evil there."

Chuckling, Trisha smacked me on the arm. "Well, if anyone can handle it, it's you, right?"

IT ENDED UP TAKING a good hour to get to the LAPD precinct where Sergeant Thompson worked. L.A. traffic was a bitch on the best of days, even more so this close to lunchtime.

My stomach grumbled, reminding me that I needed sustenance soon. My eyes caught sight of a burger place off to the side of the police station. I wanted to stop over there for a few moments, but Trisha had been pretty insistent about Thompson needing to see me right now.

To eat now or later?

My stomach yelled again. Well, I knew what its vote was.

Sighing, I climbed out of Sid's truck. The inside of it smelled like him, of whiskey and something dark and musky and so him. I swallowed pushing back the tightness in my throat.

Get it together, Mary. I sucked in a breath and clenched my jaw, my hand going to my gun under my arm. Gripping the butt of the gun until my hand ached, I slammed the door shut and marched toward the precinct, the burger joint tempting me with the scent of cooked meat all the way.

The inside was as bustling as ever with a lengthy line of people hanging around the waiting area. Some of them were no doubt there to bail someone out. Maybe pay off a ticket. Or, if the cuffs attached to the bench were any indication, waiting to be processed. The last part was a bit more unusual than the others.

"Busy day?" I asked the woman at the front desk, a snooty woman named Ester who never cared for me much. I leaned against the edge of the front desk, my eyes scanning the room with growing boredom. It was all for show though. Standing in the very room set my teeth on edge. I didn't even have to use my powers to feel the evil spilling out from inside some of those around me pretending poorly to be human.

An annoyed grunt pulled my attention back to the woman before me. Her looks weren't anything to write home about, plain as the day was long. I wouldn't have been able to pick her out of a line up even if I tried. Probably why she covered up her plainness with large dangling earrings and a scowl.

"Now, aren't you the observant one?"

Not sure what else to say, I waited and smacked my lips together. "So, can I go back?"

Her hazel eyes rolled up to look at me, exasperated that I had once again interrupted what looked like - if the shirtless man and buxom woman were anything to go by - a romance novel. "Do you have an appointment?"

I lifted a shoulder. "Not that I know of. Thompson—" She glared at me, and I quickly changed my words. "Sergeant Thompson called several times wanting my assistance."

She turned her eyes back to the book in her hand before lazily flipping the page. "And when was that?"

My brows furrowed. I didn't know. Trisha had been on my case to come down here for several days. I'd been too wrapped up in my own hunts to keep track of when exactly it had started.

"I'm not sure. I can call my assistant." I pulled my phone out and prepared to call Trisha.

Ester put her hand up, stopping me from dialing her. "That won't be necessary."

"It won't?"

"No," she clipped. "Because I have been instructed that by no uncertain circumstances am I to allow you in the back. So, consider yourself unwelcome here." She leaned forward and smiled tightly. "Have a wonderful day."

Frowning, I tucked my phone back into my back pocket and headed for the door. I didn't bother arguing with her. I'd have to wait until Thompson called me again and tell him about the new guard dog.

Unfortunately, not being welcome wasn't something exactly new to me but losing the police force from my roster of resources would make things difficult, to say the least. I'd have to rely on Trisha's exceptional skills to get me the information I needed for the Barnes case. Something I loathed to do. Putting my assistant in harm's way - whether physically or legally - turned my stomach. I'd already failed to keep her safe once I would hate to do it again. However, I didn't see much of a choice, and I knew Trisha would kick my ass if I even suggested leaving her out of it.

Sighing with annoyance, I shot one more look at Ester. She glanced up at me and made a showing motion with her hand. Letting out a huff, I turned for the door once more. However, before I could get out of the double glass doors a man near the door, chained to a bench, hissed at me.

"They're gonna whip your boy until his skin comes clean off his bones. Not even close to what that traitor deserves for consorting with an angel whore like you." He spat on the ground beside me, and I paused.

Tattooed from head to toe, his balding head could have been dirty, or it could have been more ink. It was hard to tell which one from where I stood. I dropped the veil between myself and what kept me from seeing into the souls of those around me. If the exterior of the human the demon was housed up in wasn't unpleasant enough, the swirling pit of black swirling around inside of him, its teeth gnashing at the soul inside would have been enough to deter anyone.

The demon's words shouldn't have bothered me. I was used to the taunts of demons. I'd been called worse names, even by humans, but for some reason, just the way he spoke of Sid made my skin tighten and my blood pulse with rage.

Changing my trajectory, I pounded the two steps it took to stand over him. My hand shot out and latched onto his throat. My other hand pulled my gun without thinking, the barrel of it pressed to his head before he could blink. The demon beneath me stiffened but only so slightly, his lips curling even further into a sneer.

Someone close by shouted out but didn't interfere. Probably too afraid I'd turn on them next. I never took my eyes off the demon scum.

"That won't even hurt," the demon inside chuckled until I tightened my grip, cutting off his words as he struggled to breathe.

Giving him a full tooth smile, I pressed my gun harder into his temple. "Holy bullets, asshole. And you're right, I won't feel a thing."

I watched with great satisfaction as his eyes widened and real fear filled them. I didn't usually attack demons in the middle of the police station. It was kind of bad for my whole human persona, but today was not a good day, and I really wanted to see his guts splattered in the wall.

Before I could make my dream a reality, hands gripped my arms and yanked me away from him. I fought against the two officers trying to restrain me. I threw my arms back using just enough force to throw them off me. I followed up with a swing of my fists, shoving one of the officers into a pair of screeching prostitutes. The other cop tried to pull his baton on me, but I kicked it from his hand and then whipped my body around to hit him in the chest with the heel of my boot.

The shouts in the waiting area combined with the blood pounding in my ears made it so that I didn't hear Thompson yelling at me until he was in my face. I couldn't stop my fist from flying toward his face in time, but luckily, he expected it and shifted his body so that it landed on his shoulder. A wince spread through his aged face, and I immediately regretted it.

"Dammit, Wiles, it's me." He rubbed his shoulder with an agitated frown. His gun holster strained around the large set of his shoulders. Even for a man in his fifties, he still had a form that would intimidate the strongest of mortal men. Thankfully, I was neither a man nor mortal.

Breathing heavily, I bent down to pick up my gun which had dropped in the struggle. The cocking of multiple guns stopped me. I slowly shifted my head to the side to see half a dozen officers surrounding us with guns drawn and a few civilians pointing their phones our way. Probably snapping pictures or videos to upload to social media later.

"Keep your hands where we can see them, Wiles," a smug voice commanded me, and I resisted the urge to flip them off just for the hell of it.

Officer Riley has been the bane of my existence ever since he had grown an interest in my people and me. He was determined to find some reason to have me behind bars. He'd actually accomplished that a few months ago, but Adara had the Phoenix Guild pull some strings and I was out before Riley could really get his claws into me.

"Riley, she didn't mean anything by it." Thompson held his hands up as if trying to placate a rabid dog. I didn't like the way he was looking at Riley, like he was the one calling the shots and not the other way around.

"When I want your opinion, I'll ask for it, Thompson," Riley snapped and then slowly smiled at me. "And I don't think Miss Wiles ever does anything she doesn't mean. Isn't that right?"

I gave Thompson a look and shrugged. Riley wasn't wrong.

"So, then." Riley clicked his tongue and placed his hands on his hips as he rocked back and forth on his heels. "That means we have one account of attempted murder," - he pointed a finger at the demon who had the good sense not to laugh - "one account of resisting arrest, and three accounts of assaulting a police officer."

"I'm not pressing charges." Thompson stepped forward, his large form and commanding tone not doing the usual job of intimidating those around him. Well, the other officers shifted uncomfortably but not Riley. He seemed even more of a pretentious asshole than before if that were possible.

"Well, that's not really up to you, now is it?" Riley snarled at Thompson before shoving past him to stand in front of me. He looked me up and down. The lust in his eyes was not entirely about my body though I was sure from past experience that was part of it. The majority of it was because he had me. Riley had me exactly where he has wanted me since the first time he pulled me into that interrogation room so many months ago.

"You are going to go to jail for a very long time, Miss Wiles." Riley chortled, crossing his arms over his chest. "You see, you might be fooling some of the officers around here but not me. I know what you really are."

"And what's that?" I smirked up at him curious to know what he really thought of me. I highly doubted any of his thoughts ranged to the cosmic level.

He leaned in close so I could feel his breath on my face. It smelled like the stale coffee I knew they served in the back. The words that came out of his mouth were slow and full of feeling, almost like he was telling me he loved me in a weird twisted way.

"You're a cold-blooded murderer."

I huffed a laugh and continued to pick up my gun. The officers around me tensed, and I held a hand up with a smile. "Don't worry, boys. I only hunt monsters. Your pretty faces are safe." I started to tuck my gun back into its holster, but Riley's hand gripped mine tightly. I gave him a tight grin. "If you are smart, you'd take your hands off me, Officer Riley."

Riley gave me a nasty grin, his grip tightening. "That's Lieutenant Riley to you, Miss Wiles. And I do believe I said you were under arrest. Why would I let you keep your firearm?"

I cocked my head to the side. "Are you?" My eyes slid over to Sergeant Thompson and then back to Lieutenant Riley. So that was why Thompson was letting Riley ass face call the shots. "You made Lieutenant? That's pretty impressive. Especially, for someone who was acting as an errand boy not too long ago. Whose ass did you have to kiss? Or more like whose dick did you suck? That is the right terminology, isn't it?" I glanced to Thompson once more who shook his head in disappointment.

I didn't see the fist coming. I really should have. I deserved it. I prodded the bear. What did I expect? A slap on the back?

Blood and pain filled my mouth as my face jerked to the side. Laughing through the pain, I spat on the ground. If I thought the people in the waiting room were social media crazed before, nothing compared to the sound of pictures snapping.

I grinned up at Riley. "Well, look at that. I don't think your new promotion will last very long."

"And why is that?" Riley snapped as he tucked my gun into his pants. I didn't remember him even taking it from me. He didn't wait for my answer as he started to notice the waiting room full of people staring at us. "Shut those off! You. Confiscate those cell phones."

The surrounding officers tried to do as he said but stopped as Sergeant Thompson snorted. "Too late for that. The image of the new Lieutenant of the LA police force beating a woman in the middle of the precinct is now live for everyone to see." His large arms crossed over his chest, and his chin raised slightly, a disgusted expression on his face.

"Fucking hell." Riley glared at Thompson and then at the waiting room of people who were reluctantly giving up their phones. Turning his fury filled eyes back to me, he pointed a finger at my face. "This isn't over. Don't think for a second this gets you off."

As Riley stomped away, I called out to him, "You have my gun."

Riley paused, and only half glanced over his shoulder before growling and stalking to the back.

Sighing, I ran a hand through my tangled mess of curls. "I really liked that gun." The demon possessing the man from before snickered. My eyes locked onto him making his laughter catch in his throat. "Don't think I need a gun to kill your ass."

The demon smirked, and I stepped toward him. A hand on my shoulder stopped me, and I slowly turned my head to Thompson. "That's enough for today."

"But he's a demon," I whispered harshly.

Nodding, Thompson gestured to one of the officers. "Get that guy into a cell. Alone." To me, Thompson said, "Come on, let's get you out of here before you cause a media frenzy."

INSTEAD OF LEADING ME into the back of
the police precinct, Thompson walked me
over to the burger place across the street.
How he knew that I was starving, I didn't
know how, but my stomach thanked him.

We ordered our food and sat at a table
toward the back. Thompson took the chair
facing the door, leaving me the one across
from him. Every time we went somewhere, he
did this. I wasn't sure if it was a cop thing or
if he was simply cautious by nature. I'd never
found having my eyes on the door much
help. If someone were going to attack you,
they wouldn't bother going for the obvious

entrance. Not that many humans bothered me in any case, but they were predictable. Demons weren't that polite.

Picking up my burger, I took a big mouthful and chewed slowly enjoying the taste of it before looking to Thompson. "So, Riley's your boss now? How the hell did that happen?"

Thompson dipped a French fry in ketchup and then popped it into his mouth with a shrug. "Riley broke up some big drug chain and then kissed the right amount of ass. A Lieutenant position had come up recently, and he beat me to it."

I snorted. "Figures." I grabbed my cup and sucked on the straw, using the liquid inside to wash down the burger. Grabbing a napkin from the middle of the table, I wiped my hands and mouth. When finished, I laced my fingers in front of me and met Thompson's gaze. "Are we done with the idle chitchat? I have things to do."

Thompson's lips pursed as he studied me. It was as if he was seeing me for the first time and it made me bristle. I shifted in my seat, feeling awkward. Too light without the weight of my gun at my side. It gave me flashbacks to when I lost my wings. At least, this one had less emotional and physical scarring to go along with it.

When I didn't break under Thompson's scrutinizing gaze, he dropped his hands to the table with a scowl. "What the hell is your problem? You come into the police station with a bug up your ass and even go so far as to assault someone—"

"A demon."

"And several officers." Thompson pointed out with a disappointed frown. "You used to be so careful, and here you are not giving a rat's ass who sees you."

I shoved a handful of fries in my mouth so I wouldn't have to answer right away. I knew what was wrong with me, but I couldn't tell Thompson about the rage inside of me. The helpless feeling, I couldn't get rid of. Instead, I did what I always do when I was backed into a corner.

"My methods are my own. You let me worry about the demons, you just worry about your little humans." I sucked down my drink once more slamming the cup down on the table.

I knew I wasn't being fair. I'd brought Thompson into this mess. He'd been better off without knowing about what really went bump in the night. When Asmodeus came to Earth and started to make his play for power, I'd needed back up. Stupidly, I'd asked Thompson and some other officers to be my backup. I regretted it ever since.

Thompson stared at me for a moment as if he couldn't believe the words coming out of my mouth. Hell, even I didn't sometimes. He leaned back in his seat, his arms crossing over his chest. "Well, excuse me for trying to save lives, your high and mightiness."

I slammed my hands on the table, my teeth clenched tight. "And you don't think I am? I have bigger problems than helping the police with a job they're supposed to be doing. I have enough on my plate without you and every other poor-is-me human coming to me for help. I might be an angel, but I'm no freaking saint."

"People are dying," Thompson snapped, his eyes flashing with anger. A vein pulsated in his neck, and I almost thought he might hit me. It should have been enough to make me back off but call me a masochist.

"People die every day, Thompson. You're human, that's what you do. Die." My fingers tightened along the edge of the table. "Bigger things are going on than your little murder cases. World-changing matters." And the only man I ever cared for being tortured as we spoke.

Some might think that Sidney shouldn't be my main priority, but he was only part of the equation, only one of the reasons I needed into Hell. Asmodeus had Michael's dagger, the very object with the ability to cut the fabrics of space and time, opening a door between our world and theirs. Thankfully, only an archangel can use the dagger but who's saying that Asmodeus didn't have another one of those in his pocket? He had Ramiel after all.

Before you killed him. A nagging voice reminded me. I shoved the voice and the guilt aside. I had bigger problems than my conscience.

Of course, the thought of my ex-friend and boss made the helplessness I was feeling even worse. It was like I was back in Hell, chained to the stone table, the demons cackling at me as they hacked away my wings. I had promised myself I'd never feel that way again, unable to do anything but let them rip into me. This was worse though because this time, instead of the knife cutting into me, it was the inability to save someone I loved.

Thompson cleared his throat kicking me out of my thoughts. I glanced up from my burger to see him shake his head. "I can't say anything for world-changing matters. All I can do is my job, and last time I checked, solving murders were part of your job too."

I sighed and tapped the tabletop with my nails. "Not anymore. I don't have time. I'm sorry."

Breathing in deeply, Thompson let out a disappointed grunt. "Then I guess we are through here." Gathering up the files on the table I hadn't given him the chance to show me, he stood. He started toward the door but then stopped and stomped back to our table, pointing a finger at me. "You know, I never used to believe in the supernatural. I knew there was bad shit in this world and accepted it but then you, fuck, you opened my eyes to a whole new world of possibilities. Horrible keep-you-up-at-night possibilities."

"That's not my problem!" I lowered my voice as I started to attract an audience. "In case you forgot, I'm not human. Your problems are not mine."

Thompson's face puffed up, and his skin practically turned purple. "Well, I'm making it your problem. You might have larger-than-life issues, but I live here, in the now, and right now, we have people dying. Whole families."

He chucked the folder at me, pictures falling out onto the table. Bodies torn to shreds with blood puddled beneath them filled every page. I stared down at them with a hollow feeling inside. Even when I found a page with a corpse so small, I thought for a moment that it might be one half of a whole, but then I saw the teddy bear. Its fur was matted and colored a reddish brown.

The feeling that hit me hit me hard. My throat clogged with emotion, and my eyes burned for the tiny being on the glossy image in front of me. Death hadn't bothered me before. I'd seen worse crime scene photos than this. Why this one? Why this photo?

Pushing down the emotions, I slowly stacked the images into a pile, putting the one of the child on top. I closed the folder without another look and cleared my throat.

I wished I could leave it alone. That I could shove that feeling I had at seeing the child mutilated down and tell Thompson no, but I couldn't. I didn't know if it was the human part of me that kept creeping in or if it's my angel side. We're supposed to be compassionate and caring, right? God's little servants to look over mankind in his stead. That's what I'm supposed to be, right?

I glanced up at Thompson and saw the anger and disgust on his face. The pure rage for who or what did this to these people. "Tell me about the pictures." Even to me, my voice was empty, void of emotion. Trisha would cry. I knew she would, but I couldn't. Not yet.

Thompson sat back down across from me. He took the folder and tapped it on the table. "This is the fourth set of bodies in the last month. I'm surprised you haven't heard of it. The media has been all over it."

I lifted a shoulder. "I don't watch much television. Most nights I don't get home until almost dawn."

"Hunting..." Thompson lowered his voice his eyes skittering from side to side before finally saying, "... demons?"

"Yeah."

"And how's that going for you?" Thompson shifted in his seat his eyes suddenly more interested in my life than the deaths of those in the pictures. Not that I blamed him. I'd rather think about anything than the victims in the folder.

"Not well," I admitted, shaking my head. "Most of the demons I find are low ranked. They don't know crap and only want to taunt me."

"Like today?"

I sniffed and smirked. "Yeah, the word has spread of Sid's capture faster than cancer. They know I'm looking for them and what I want. If they do know how to get into Hell, they aren't telling. Not that I blame them." I cupped my soda cup in my hands, letting the cold contents of it chill my hands. I welcomed the numbing sensation. It was better than the overbearing emotions.

Thompson gave me a sympathetic look and his brows furrowed. "I really wish I could help you out, but gateways to Hell are not exactly something the police are experts in."

"I didn't expect you to be." I rubbed a hand over my face, wanting this all to be over. I couldn't remember ever being this tired, this worn out, in Heaven. "But you're right. I got you into this, and I should at least do my part to keep the rest of the world from going to shit while I try to keep the demons in Hell."

"I appreciate it. More than you know." He inclined his head toward the file. "So, what do you think?"

"About what?" I quirked a brow.

"The pictures. Are they demonic?" He held the file up like that would make everything clearer.

My face scrunched up, and I shrugged. "How should I know?"

"You can't tell?" his voice raised an octave as if it were the most insane thing he'd ever heard.

I grabbed the folder and flipped it open to show the image that made my heart ache. "This is only blood and gore." I gestured a hand over the picture, forcing myself not to see the image as a whole. "No ritual, no symbols. Not that all demons used those things but if there are multiple killings there's usually a reason. Most demons simply kill for the sake of killing but they are usually cleaner about it. You get good at covering your tracks after a while."

Thompson gave me a curious look that made me realize what I'd just said. No need to let on to him my less than extracurriculars.

"These pictures are only of the bodies, not the whole crime scene. I mean, if you'd taken me to one of them, I might be able to figure something out, but this won't tell me if it was a demon or otherwise. I mean, why would you think that it was a demon? It could just have easily been a human."

"That can't be right." Thompson shook his head, anxiety filling his face. "If it was human, then why would four whole families be butchered like this? A human couldn't do this, could they?"

I leveled a look at him. "Couldn't they? You're a cop. You of all people should know what people are capable of."

"I guess as an angel you know that as well." He huffed a laugh. "By the way, I have questions about that like Heaven and other things." I snorted, and Thompson smiled. It was short lived though, when the weight of the file in front of him came back. Thompson sighed, and a sense of despair came over him. "I was so hoping it was demons."

I lifted a shoulder and gave him a reassuring curl of my lips. "It still could be. Maybe the demon possesses one of the family members, kills them then the host, and moves on to the next one. Though, that sounds like a lot more work than it was worth to me. Most demons would rather corrupt the family and watch them slowly destroy themselves. More fun that way."

"That's a good point." Thompson pulled out a tiny notepad from his breast pocket and started to scribble down notes. "And are there any signs to look out for? To know if the demon is possessing these people?"

I smiled slightly at how eager he looked to get information from me. Maybe I should just write a book, *How to Identify and Kill Demons* by Muriel, Archangel of God. Oh, yeah. I could see me on the bestseller list now.

Not explaining my amusement, I leaned forward in my seat. "Well, most demons can't hop from body to body that fast. It wears them out. Usually, when they pick a body, they stay for a while."

"Until someone like you comes and kicks them out?" Thompson pointed his pen at me a bit smug, I couldn't help but smirk.

"Right, but as far as signs?" I scratched my face as I thought about the first signs. "If a demon possesses someone, they might start missing work. Irregular mood swings. You know, things out of character. Most don't get violent right away. They have to get used to their new form." And fight the soul they were suffocating with their presence, but I didn't tell him about that part. Some things were better left unsaid.

"This is all good stuff. Really good stuff. The families that were killed all happened in the same neighborhood, so we thought it was someone who lived there." Thompson finished scribbling his notes before shoving it back into his pocket.

I nodded. "That makes sense. The demon might be house jumping."

My phone started to buzz in my pocket. I pulled it out and glanced at the screen. Adara. Finally.

Shooting a look at Thompson, I said, "I've got to take this. Do you need anything else?"

Thompson shook his head and stood. "I'm good. I'll have the guys search for someone acting oddly and out of character. Want me to let you know if we find someone?"

As I pushed the answer button, I nodded. "Sounds good. Hey, Adara. Tell me you have something for me."

5

ADARA ASKED ME TO meet her at Phoenix Guild headquarters. It was located in one of the nicer parts of L.A. in a large mansion surrounded by wrought iron fences. They even had a guard man at the door waiting to turn away the unwanted.

The guard glanced over my ID and stared at me as if he could see into my soul. Well, keep looking, buddy, because you won't find one. One of the perks and downfalls of being an angel. When I go, I'm gone.

When the guard finally deemed me worthy to pass, he handed me back my ID without a word and pushed a button in his little guard box.

"Thanks." I offered him a small nod, and because I'm one of those people who just can't help themselves, I added, "Security sure has gotten better since I broke into this place a while ago."

The guard's eyes narrowed, but he didn't respond. Pity. Trisha would have been proud.

Pulling Sid's truck up to the front of the mansion, I scanned over the place. The Phoenix Guild was a group of humans who were born with heightened senses and a tattoo across their back of their namesake. They were the human - well as human as they could get - version of me. Hunting demons and keeping mankind safe with no thanks or a paycheck.

It was how Adara found me. She was hunting some demons in the woods and came across my passed-out, tortured form. Adara nursed me back to health and taught me the ways of the human world, even got me my own set of identification. Which was how I went from Muriel, archangel of God, to Mary Wiles, Private Investigator.

However, while Adara might be a Phoenix, she hadn't been part of the guild for a long time, not since her father killed her vampire lover. Irony at its best.

"Hey, come on in." Adara opened the door to the large mansion. The foyer was filled with display cases which I knew were filled with ancient artifacts and weapon. An empty one still stood in the middle of the room where Michael's blade once sat. Trisha and I had tried to steal it once upon a time, but we turned out to be lousy thieves.

"You know, I'm surprised you wanted to meet here." I followed behind her to a room off to the left of the foyer. There were even more weapons displayed in here as well as walls full of books.

Adara sat down behind a large oak desk, flipping her long dark braid over her shoulder. She actually had sensible clothing on for once. Usually, Adara looked like she was ready to party all night long, but today she wore a button-down white shirt and black slacks. She was downright proper.

"Yeah, I know, but my father's been trying to make amends, and I'm..." she drew out and took in a sharp breath before letting it out.

75

"Holding on by a thread? Tired of pretending to be something you're not?" I offered up as I moved over to the wall of books. I thumbed over the titles only half paying attention what I was reading.

Barking a laugh, Adara rubbed a hand over her face. "Fuck me. I hate this crap. I hate dressing up like I have a stick in my ass. Getting up at the crack of dawn, kissing the asses of the old coots who run the council."

"I thought your father ran the whole thing? Where's he at?" I twisted around to see her. She looked two seconds away from pounding her face into the desk.

"He's... not doing so well." Her voice grew low and childlike. It was then that I noticed the dark circles under her eyes. The lines along her mouth that weren't there before. She'd aged at least five years since the last time I saw her.

"What happened?" I moved around the desk and placed my hand on her shoulder. I didn't always know when to say the right thing, human sentiment wasn't really built into my angelic genes, but it was clear Adara was under a lot of stress. That warranted interest in her and her family. See? Who said I wasn't learning?

76

Adara's hand touched mine, and she squeezed it slightly. "It's a combination of things. Failing heart and all the stress that comes with being the head of a secret demon-hunting organization." She snort-laughed, but it sounded bitter. "Can you imagine? A demon hunter dying from clotted arteries instead of in the field?"

I gave her a soft smile. "I bet he's hating every second of it."

"And raising hell even now." She shook her head and rubbed her eyes before sniffing. She picked up a folder on the desk and held it up to me. Taking the folder from her hands, I walked back around the desk to sit in one of the visitor's chairs. "I found a woman in SoCal that claims to be able to create portals to other dimensions."

"Claims?" I looked up from the file that had a picture of an older woman in her fifties. She had tight red curls and soulful eyes. I had a feeling if I met this woman in person she would know right away I was different, like Madame Serena had.

The door to the office opened suddenly, revealing an attractive looking man in a suit. The bright blue eyes behind thick-rimmed glasses locked onto me the moment he stepped into the room. A hunter, I could tell by the analyzing look in his eyes. Like he was trying to figure out if he would have to kill me and how.

"My apologies, Adara, I thought you were alone." He sort of half bowed to Adara which made my lip tick up at the side. I raised a brow at my friend who ignored me and pursed her lips.

"What do you want, Alec?" Woah. The only time I heard that tone was when Adara was hunting, something she hadn't done in a long time. Well, not on her own. She spent more time having intercourse with demons than actually killing them. And people said I had issues.

My eyes shot from Adara to the hunter now known as Alec. His back straightened, and his fingers curled into fists at his side, but that was the only sign that he noticed her scorching glare. I sensed a bit of history between them, like he wasn't too happy with her being in charge or that he had to take orders from her.

"I have those reports you wanted from last night's hunt." Alec put his hands behind his back, but I didn't see the so-called reports he had mentioned.

Adara didn't seem too bothered by it. "You can drop them by later." She gestured her head toward the door, clearly dismissing him and then looked back to the desk, shuffling things around that didn't need to be shuffled.

Alec either didn't realize he was being dismissed or didn't care because he didn't move. Well, well. This was more interesting than the shows Trisha made me watch. At least, there were no commercials.

"Was there anything else?" The sharpness to Adara's tone said it all. It said, 'I don't give a crap what you want, get the hell out of my face.' Man, I wish I had some popcorn. That's what people usually ate during movies, right?

Clearing his throat, Alec pressed his lips tightly together. "I was under the impression that you wanted a full briefing as soon as possible."

Adara's head jerked up. Giving him a nasty grin, Adara clasped her hands in front of her on the desk. "I know what I said but as you can see," - she gestured a hand toward me - "I'm busy. You can come back later—"

"But—"

"—or I could shove those reports so far up your ass, you'll be shitting them out until Christmas," Adara snapped back at him, and even I flinched. I had to hand it to her. The visual she created would make a demon proud. Not so much Alec, who took her threats in stride.

"Fine." He inclined his head slightly, almost as if he were bowing to her. Hilarious because the expression on his face said Alec would rather kick her ass than kiss it. "I'll come back later."

"You do that."

When Alec left, I leaned back in my chair and grinned. "That was a bit harsh. What was that?" I gestured my chin toward the door where Alec had closed behind him.

"What? He's a dick," Adara muttered and then scribbled something on the paper in front of her. I watched her with growing interest, my hands laying on my stomach as I waited for her to break. Eventually, my silence got to her, as I knew it would. Slapping her pen down, she locked her eyes with mine. "What do you want me to say?"

I lifted a shoulder. "I don't know. Just wondering what that poor guy could have done to warrant such violence from only wanting to do his job?"

Adara snorted. "More like trying to tell me how to do mine." I cocked my head to the side, making Adara sigh. "Alec is the one my father had been grooming to take his spot as head of the guild. Until..."

"You came back into the fold." I nodded, understanding the animosity between them.

"Right. So, of course, he hates my guts, and he's not the only one." Adara shifted in her seat before picking her pen back up and scribbling some more.

"Well, I see you're up to your ears in paperwork, so I'll just take this," - I stood and held the folder up - "and be on my way."

"Ah, ah, ah," Adara called out to me before I could get two steps toward the door.

"What?"

Adara stood, coming around the desk to cut me off. "I didn't give that to you so that you could go off on your own. I'll come with you."

I frowned. "You don't have to do that. I can handle one little old lady."

Crossing her arms over her chest, she sniffed. "I'm sure you can, but I don't want that little old lady to end up a little old dead lady. Especially one that I pointed you at. That's the last thing I need for my rep right now."

"And when did you give a crap about your reputation? You were screwing vamps and demons left and right up until recently. Giving a big ol' middle finger to your old man and now you're here telling me not to get out of hand?" Shaking my head, I started to push past her, but her hand clamped down on my shoulder.

"I'm not letting you go alone, Mary."

I curled my fingers into a fist and clenched my jaw. "I'm not going to kill her. I'm just going to talk to her."

Adara tightened her grip on my shoulder. "Like you talked to that woman the other night? If talking with you ends with a bullet hole in the head, I'm not sure you're doing it right."

"Who told you about that?" My heart beat in my chest at the mention of the demon I'd taken out in the middle of an interrogation. I didn't usually let those evil bastards get to me, but it seemed I was a bit touchy as of late.

"You're getting sloppy. My guys on the force were on call last night when you made the call. They were out hunting a pack of vamps. You're lucky they found her and not Riley's guys." Adara dropped her hand from me and shifted toward the door. "Plus, Trisha called me."

At the mention of Riley, I grimaced. The guy was really asking for some divine intervention. I frowned at the thought of Trisha tattling on me to Adara. Following Adara out the office door, I adjusted my spare gun in my holster. "It was nothing. Just some low-rank demon that didn't know when to shut up."

"And that warrants killing them?" she said over her shoulder on her way to a large set of double doors near a few cases of holy relics. The first pope's hat. A nail from the crucifixion. How they got all these things wasn't too surprising. The guild had been around for almost as long as man has been civilized, waiting on the shadows to take out the evils hunting their brethren.

The doors Adara opened had a dozen or so black garments lined in a row, each one with a name above them. Hanging next to them were gun holsters and knives, different weapons for each person. Adara unbuttoned her white shirt and tossed it into the small bench beneath her name. If disrobing in the middle of the mansion seemed to bother her, she didn't show it. One thing we had in common, among others.

My eyes trailed over the black phoenix tattoo which spread across her back like a badge of honor. I wanted to reach out and touch it, see if it was like any other tattoo or if it was ingrained into her skin like a birthmark. But I never would. I knew better than to overstep my bounds like that. It would be like someone asking to touch the scars on my back where my wings had been sawed off at the quick. I shuddered, my head turning to the side in suppressed pain.

As Adara pulled a black tank top on and began to strap on her gun and wrist sheaths, I moved into the closet. "I didn't mean to put a bullet in her head. I had every intention of exorcizing the demon."

"So, the soul was still alive in her?" Adara glanced up from the strap on her thigh holster.

Her question made me grimace. One of my abilities as an angel was the ability to see one's soul, even those who were being possessed by demons. Most humans don't survive a demon possession, they aren't strong enough to resist or push them out. Though there were a few lucky ones that I could save by exorcizing the demon. However, what was left behind... they might not say I did them any favors.

My lips twisted, and I didn't meet her gaze. "I didn't check." It was a lie, but I hoped she wouldn't notice.

"You didn't check?" Adara scoffed, and I chanced a glance back at her. She shook her head as she pulled her leather jacket on. "That's not like you at all, Mare."

"I know." I sighed, already getting tired of the questions and we still had a long drive ahead of us. I could only imagine how many more I would be subjected to.

"Maybe you're losing your touch." She closed the door with a firm snap and started toward the door.

"Or my mind." I trailed after her with nothing but a cloud of gloom following after me.

THE DRIVE TO LONG Beach was a quiet one. Neither one of us had much to say. Most likely because we were both stuck in our own thoughts and didn't have much interest in talking to one another. With everything going on with Adara's father and taking over the Phoenix guild it wasn't surprising she'd be so preoccupied. The fact that she was even helping me with how much she already had on her plate was a testament to our friendship.

Or how little she trusted me.

Not that I really blamed her. The last few months had been hard on all of us, not just me. However, I was the one who was floundering. Taking my anger and helplessness out on any and every one I could get my hands on, no matter how much I hurt them. Honestly, I was surprised I only had Adara to babysit me and not the whole guild.

"When we get there let me do the talking," Adara announced suddenly as we pulled off the interstate.

I turned my head toward her and frowned. "Why? Do you think I'll say something to offend her?"

Lifting one shoulder, Adara readjusted her hands on the wheel. "No, I don't think you will say something, I know you will. You have a habit of putting your foot in your mouth. Especially, when it comes to social niceties."

I scoffed. "I do not." Adara shot me a look. "Okay, so maybe I don't quite a hundred percent get your human customs, but I still try my best to abide by them." She stared at me hard, this time lifting a brow. I sighed and shook my head. "I'm not going to go in their guns blazing and demand she takes me to Hell or else."

"Well, that's a relief." Adara rolled her eyes and turned back to the road. The GPS said we were only a few minutes away from this person's house and I could feel the anxiety creeping in. This could be it. In a few short minutes, I could have my portal to Hell and my ticket to saving Sid.

"This is it," Adara proclaimed, and I barely waited for Adara's SUV to stop before I jumped out of the car. Adara shouted after me as I strode across the lawn.

The house was small it couldn't have been more than a one bedroom and was painted a pale robin egg blue. A cluster of palm trees stood in the middle of the lawn providing some much-needed shade.

The sound of wind chimes filled my ears as my feet landed on the porch. The woman had lined them up and down the side of the house adding uniqueness to the plain house.

I stopped my trek to stare at them for a moment. The wind chimes were not like others I'd seen. They weren't made of metal or decorated with ridiculous babbles. Or worse shaped like animals. These were made of wood and bones. They whistled as the wind blew through them. I stepped toward them to take a closer look when Adara landed on the porch next to me, breathing heavily.

"Don't do that," she gasped at me, and I wondered how she could have gotten so out of shape so fast. Ignoring her for a moment, I turned back to the wind chimes. A power resonated from them that seemed familiar, but I couldn't quite place.

When I reached a finger out to touch them, a voice stopped me. "Unless you want to get a shock of your lifetime, I wouldn't do that if I were you."

The voice had come from the woman from the file. She leaned on a cane made of the same kind of wood as her wind chimes, and her dress billowed around her like it a butterfly's wings, the multicolored fabric flapping in the wind. The tight curls on her head were now looser and hung down to her shoulders, the bright red dulled and sprinkled with gray hairs. The picture Adara had must have been at least a decade old. This woman was practically ancient to most humans.

"Thank you for the warning." I nodded and started toward her. "You must be Octavia. I'm—"

"Muriel, yes, I know." Octavia nodded and then pointed her cane at Adara. "And you're the new head of the Phoenix Guild, Adara Ashwood."

"How do you know who we are?" Adara asked, suspicious filling her voice as her hand crept to her gun. I didn't bother reaching for mine. This woman didn't mean us any harm. It only took me a fraction of a second to glimpse into Octavia's soul and confirm that. Pure and white, like newly fallen snow.

Octavia sniffed. "I wasn't born yesterday, my little hunter. Now come in before we let the bugs in the house. We have a lot to discuss, you and I." Her eyes were on me, not Adara when she spoke. We followed her into the house, and Adara closed the door behind us.

Inside there was a faint scent of mothballs and incense as if she had walked the house with burned sage. It was something Madame Serena would have done and only added to this woman's intrigue. The living room furniture filled every corner of the room leaving hardly any walking room. I didn't think much of the loud floral print on them, but Adara's face clearly showed she didn't like it here. Must be her father's influence on her.

"Would you like some tea?" Octavia asked as we sat down, Adara on the furthest chair where she could see the door — one of those cop things — and me on the couch. Octavia didn't sit down immediately, waiting patiently for our answer.

"Sure." I smiled up at her genuinely at ease in her home.

"None for me thanks," Adara said tightly, her discomfort apparent. When Octavia hobbled her way into the kitchen, Adara turned to me immediately. "I don't like this. That woman gives me the creeps." She rubbed her hands up and down her arms, blowing air between her lips.

I shrugged. "I don't know why. That woman could be a saint. Definitely, one of the few with a spot already marked for them in Heaven."

"You think?"

I crossed a leg over the other and leaned back into the couch. "It's easy to pretend to be good, but souls don't lie, and that woman's soul doesn't have a speck of darkness in it. So, you can relax."

92

Adara frowned not completely believing me, but she did relax slightly. Octavia came back into the living room a few moments later with a tray of tea and even little cookies. Adara for all her suspicions still stood and took the tray from her, sitting it on the coffee table between us. Octavia nodded her thanks and took a seat in the recliner across from us. We waited while she poured the tea and even though Adara had refused a cup, she placed a cup and saucer in front of her.

"Just in case you change your mind." Octavia winked at Adara before handing me my cup. Octavia started pouring some milk and sugar into her own tea and stirred it as she watched us. "So, you want to go to Hell, correct?"

"Right." I nodded, moving closer to the edge of my seat. "I need a portal into Hell to save someone, and Adara said you could make me that portal?" I watched Octavia's face expectantly, waiting for the good news we had driven all the way down here to hear. So, when the pleasant smile on her lips slowly dipped, and a seriousness covered her face, I knew what she was going to say next was not what I wanted to hear.

"You can open a portal, right?" Adara asked for me, clearly seeing what I saw. The apprehension in her posture matched mine, and it only made me more anxious.

"Well, yes... and no." Octavia sat her cup down on the table and cleared her throat. "I can open a portal, of course, but it requires several factors to come in alignment."

"Like what?" My words came out almost a shout, my patience wearing thin. "I mean, whatever you need we can get it. Right Adara?" I glanced to my friend, sure that she could use the guild's resources to find whatever we needed or even pull some big favor for this.

"Yes." Adara nodded, cautiously. "Please just let us know what you need, and we will get it. It won't be an issue."

Octavia smiled at Adara, adjusting the watch on her wrist. "That is very kind of you, but the factors are not all materialistic. This ritual requires a full moon as well as something that is as dangerous as going to Hell."

"Okay, a full moon is fine." I counted up the days quickly in my head. "That's only a few days. No problem. What's the other part?

Whatever it is, I'll do it. I have to get Sid back, I have to."

Octavia exchanged a look with Adara, one that said I might be acting a bit desperate. Which I knew I was and didn't care. I would do anything to not only get Sid back but to get my wings and the dagger. Everything I need and want is in Hell. The irony of it was not lost on me either.

"Are you sure this is something you want to do?" Octavia slowly said, sitting her hands on her knees as she leaned toward me. "This isn't something that you can take back later. You have to be absolutely certain beyond a shadow of a doubt that this is what you want to do."

"I am, I mean, I'm certain. I'll do whatever it takes." I clenched my jaw and sat up taller trying to show her that I wasn't going to back down.

"Very well." Octavia inclined her head slowly and then picked her teacup back up. She took a long drink before turning her attention back to me. "First, before we open the portal I think it best if you make sure you find what you are looking and make sure it is still there for you to save."

My brow furrowed, and I glanced over at Adara. Adara shrugged, clearly as confused as I was. "How exactly do I do that without a portal?"

"Oh, I don't need a portal or a full moon for that. Only a few herbs would do."

"And what do those do?" Adara asked. I was glad she did because I was at the point where I didn't care what it took. I might end up dead and buried because of my rash thinking. Something that no one, especially Sid, would thank me for.

Octavia poured herself another cup of tea while I realized I hadn't even touched mine yet. "It's called astroprojection. I'll send your energy — or essence as you will — to Hell and you will use it to find your friend. Make sure this Sid is actually there waiting for you."

I shook my head. "Why? I don't see the point. We are going to Hell anyway, I don't need to get a sneak peek of what's coming. Believe me, the first time was bad enough."

"Ah, yes. I heard you had been there before. How was it?" Octavia quirked a brow as if she were merely asking me about the weather.

I scowled. "How do you think? It's Hell. Blood, torture, nightmares. Everything they say it is and more."

"Oh really? That's too bad." Octavia sighed and sat back in her chair, crossing one ankle over the other. "I have quite a few friends who are headed that way, I'd hate to see them suffer."

I couldn't help but snort. "Believe me, if they are going to Hell, it's because they deserve it. You shouldn't bother yourself with worry for them."

"Oh, but I must." A sort of twinkle filled Octavia's eye. "If I don't worry for their souls who will? They certainly don't. And just because you're ready to jump into the jaws of your fate doesn't mean those around you are ready to let you." The way she said it made me feel like she was warning me in some way. Telling me that I was being stupid and reckless. Not that I didn't know that already.

"Alright, so astroprojection. Let's do it." I nodded toward her, prepared to get it over with.

"Always in such a hurry." Octavia laughed slightly, shaking her head. "We don't have time to do it right now."

"Why not?" I asked just as my phone went off. Trisha. What could she want? "Hello?"

"Mary! Where in the holy Hell are you? Or rather Heaven but that's beside the point. Where are you right now?" Trisha's high-pitched squealing made me wince, and I glanced over at Octavia and Adara who watched in interest.

"I'm with Adara, finding my way into Hell."

"Well, I'm in hell here," Trisha whispered harshly as if someone else was in the room with her. "Mrs. Barnes is here wanting an update on their son before they leave town. I need you here now."

"That's going to be a problem since I'm an hour away from you." I shifted in my seat, not wanting to deal with my clients when I was so close to getting Sid back.

"Well, you better. Hold on one moment. Yes, this is Mary. She's stuck at a crime scene." A loud voice filled the background, and Trisha cried out, "No, don't. She'll be here soon."

98

The phone was silent for a moment, and I almost thought I lost her. "Hello?"

"Hello? Miss Wiles?" Mrs. Barnes's annoyed voice filled the line.

"Uh, yes?"

"I'm over here at your office once more without you. Now, I was under the impression you could help us, but you seem to have more important things to do than to find my son—"

"Mrs. Barnes," I tried to cut in, but she kept going.

"I'm not finished. Now, I know you don't have much of a business as it is but believe me when I say that if you don't get your butt in gear and find my son no one will ever come to you again. In fact, no one will know you for anything ever again! Am I clear?"

Brows furrowed, and jaw clenched I bit out, "Crystal."

"Then I'll see you in an hour." She didn't make it a question and hung up before I could tell her to shove it.

"What was that?" Adara asked when I hung up the phone and stood.

Scowling, I shoved my phone into my back pocket. "Come on, we have to go. My day job is interfering with my real life." Turning to Octavia, I asked, "Do you think you could come with us to LA? You could stay at my place. I mean, until we get the portal stuff all worked out?"

"She's not staying with you." Adara brushed her legs off and moved from the chair to stand beside me.

"Why not?" I frowned at her.

"Because for one, you only have one bed. Two, from the sound of it you have another pain in the ass client to deal with. Three, I don't trust you not to have demons come busting into your home." Adara ticked them off on her fingers one by one, making me frown harder.

"And they won't at yours?"

"I live in a mansion full of demon hunters. No demon in a fifty-mile radius wants to come near the guild." She placed her hand on her hip and smirked, so proud of herself.

Either Trisha was rubbing off on me, or I just couldn't help myself as I snorted and grinned. "Too bad you can't say the same thing about your bedroom."

"ARE YOU SURE YOU don't want me to drop you off at your car?" Adara put her car into park at the front of my office. "I can get Octavia set up and ready for when you come back."

"No," I bit out already irritated that my day job was once against interfering with my quest to save Sid. "I'm just going to pop up there, smooth things over, and grab Trisha."

"Do you think she needs to be there for this?" Adara glanced over her shoulder at Octavia who seemed happy as a clam simply to be out of her own house. "It might be a bit graphic."

"Do not fret over your young hacker." Octavia smiled. I didn't even bother asking how she knew that Trisha was a hacker. That's psychics for you. "She is made of stronger stuff than you think."

"See?" I pointed a thumb back at the older woman, opening the door to get out. "It'll be fine. Stop stressing."

"Says the one who got bitch slapped by Trisha's mom."

I rolled my eyes and got out of the car. My eyes skimmed over Madame Serena's dark shop. I still hadn't figured out what to do with it. I could move my office down there and then use the top half for myself. It would be nice not to have to sleep and crap where I worked.

Fiddling with my keys in my hands, I sighed. Too many things were changing, I missed the good old days where I only had to worry about cheating spouses, exorcisms, and the occasional flirting from Sid. I snorted as I walked up the stairs. Who would have thought I'd miss those days? I sure didn't. I had been so focused on getting back to Heaven back then that I didn't appreciate what I had. Though, I couldn't say I would take back how Sid and our relationship has progressed.

Thoughts of his skin pressed against mine in a torturous burning pleasure caused a shudder to run through me. No, definitely didn't regret that.

When I approached the office door, I could hear the raised voices inside. That didn't bode well. Prepared for the onslaught that was bound to happen the moment I stepped into the office, I turned the doorknob.

"I'm just saying, Mrs. Barnes, you can't expect these things to happen overnight. They take time," Trisha's exasperated voice filtered out of my office and into the reception area. I'd have to talk to her about keeping clients out of my personal space when I wasn't here. Things were beginning to feel claustrophobic without my own space. Even in Heaven, I'd had my own kind of sanctuary. The idea of moving the office downstairs was definitely becoming more and more appealing.

"And I am saying that we don't have time for your usual procedure. My boy could be lying dead in a ditch somewhere while your boss is off playing around."

"I hardly call consulting with the police playing around," I interjected as I leaned against the door frame. Trisha's eyes darted to me, relief washing over her face. Mrs. Barnes spun around her face scrunched together like a pit bull, and I swore she practically growled at me.

"You." She pointed a finger at me, marching over to where I stood. Her husband was precariously not present which meant I got the full force of this mama bears fury. "You said you'd find my boy and where do I find you? Causing a scene at the police station. How can you help me if you can't keep yourself out of jail?"

Trisha arched a brow at me, but I shook my head, telling her I'd talk about it later.

I wasn't surprised Mrs. Barnes had seen the videos that had been leaked to social media. I hadn't exactly tried to keep a low profile. My lips ticked up thinking about how pissed off Riley had to be but then forced it back. Smiling would not be a good idea in this instance.

"Mrs. Barnes." I leveled a stern look at her. "I understand your desperation."

"Desperation? I'm livid."

I held a hand up, stopping her from continuing. "Still, I said I would help you and I will. But that also means you have to trust me to get to the bottom of it my way. You can't call me every hour on the hour and expect me to hop to."

"Why, I never—"

"Yes, you did. You are stressing my assistant out and making our process take longer because we have to hand hold you." I lifted off the door frame and urged her through. "Now, please do us all a favor. Go home. Have a glass of wine, pop some pills, suck off your husband's cock whatever it is that will make you chill the fuck out because I'm done playing nice with you."

Mrs. Barnes gasped in mortification but didn't argue. Her jaw clenched, and she pulled the strap of her oversized bag tighter over her shoulder she stomped to my office door. "Just do your job, Mary Wiles, or you will regret it."

I sighed as the door shut. "I already do."

"Oh, my god," Trisha breathed, her laughter barely contained. "That was fabulous."

I cocked a brow at her. "Not going to lecture me about being professional?"

"Hell no," Trisha scoffed, flipping her black and pink streaked hair over her shoulder. "That woman is a pain in the ass. You know she has literally called the office every five minutes looking for you and an update. I had thought she'd given up when I stopped getting the calls, but then the beast of a woman showed up at the office."

"Sometimes you need hard love." I grabbed her bag from the coat stand by the door and tossed it at her. "Now, come on. Adara's waiting in the car downstairs with our ticket to Hell."

"What?" Trisha asked, hurrying after me as I exited the office. "What do you mean our ticket to Hell?"

I explained to her about Octavia on our way downstairs, Trisha asking questions all the while. When we got to the bottom of the stairs, I half expected Mrs. Barnes to be waiting and watching to see if I was doing my job. Thankfully, she wasn't, but Adara was leaning against the outside of the car, Octavia in the backseat.

"Took you long enough."

I lifted a shoulder. "Sorry, had an irate client."

She nodded to the left. "I figured the angry Betty Crocker must have been the problem." She shook her head with a grin. "I do not envy your job. Give me a late-night stakeout and blood any day over playing nice with clients."

Trisha snorted. "Like you could, you're even pricklier than Mary is when it comes to social niceties." She opened the back door and slipped into the backseat next to Octavia. "Hi, I'm Trisha."

Trisha shut the door behind her, so I didn't hear what Octavia said in reply, but I had a feeling it was probably something along the lines of 'I know.'

Turning back to Adara, I ran a hand through my hair and frowned. "Don't listen to her. You're far more level-headed than I am when faced with conflict. Probably your father's influence, right?" I offered her a laughing smile. I jumped into my side of the car before the fist she swung out could land.

"Really?" Trisha's voice had gone up a considerable amount in pitch. "You can tell all that just by looking at me?"

Octavia's eyes crinkled at the sides as she smiled mysteriously. "It's hardly a challenge."

"Is everyone ready to go?" Adara asked, climbing into the car. "I have business to attend to and won't be able to babysit you while Octavia helps you with your spirit quest."

"Spirit quest?" Trisha cocked her head to the side. "You didn't tell me about that."

I waved off the accusation in her voice. "Don't worry about it. The spirit part is hardly the worst of it."

Trisha started to argue, but Octavia interjected. "She is right. Peeking into Hell is much easier than going there. You should not worry yourself."

Letting out a dissatisfied growl, Trisha flopped back in her seat and pulled her phone out. With Trisha thoroughly emerged in her phone, I turned back to the front. "So, are you sure your father will be okay with us doing this at the guild?"

Adara's shoulders tensed. "I doubt he will even be informed. Besides, I'm in charge now. What I say goes." She cranked the car and pulled away from the curb, her hands tightly gripping the steering wheel.

Octavia chuckled in the back seat, and I exchanged a knowing grin with her. Adara might be in charge, but that didn't mean everybody was happy with the choice. The steely expression on Alec's face came to mind. I had a feeling he would have something to say about our being there, opening doorways to Hell.

The ride to the guild was over far sooner than expected, each of us thinking about our own problems. Well, except Trisha who had yet to look up from her phone. Probably playing some game.

"Here we are," Adara announced, turning in her seat to look at Octavia. "I'll show you to your room, and then we can meet in my office to do the spirit quest."

Nodding in agreement, we dispersed from the car and headed for the front door. The door opened for us as we reached it and the stiff-lipped Alec appeared.

"Ma'am," he bit out, his arms crossed over his chest. "We are overdue for that report."

"Fucking asswipe," Adara muttered under her breath but then offered Alec a tight smile. "Of course, please have Hendricks show our guest Octavia to a room." She turned her head to me. "I will talk to Alec in the war room, you can use my office for the thing we discussed."

Giving her a knowing smirk which she responded with an eye roll, I grabbed Trisha by the arm. "Come on, let's go wait in the office."

Trisha frowned, her eyes darting between Adara and Alec. Even she could see something was going on between the two of them. However, she didn't comment.

Octavia, on the other hand, did not bother with the same courtesy. "You should save everyone involved a lot of time and heartache and simply admit your attraction already. Take it from someone who has known her fair share of wasted time."

Adara gaped at the older woman as Alec stiffened. Trisha and I giggled but knew better than to hang around. Adara tended to lash out at those around her when put in an uncomfortable position. Poor Alec. He'd be getting the brunt of her anger.

Inside Adara's office, Trisha glanced around the room with big saucer-sized eyes. "Wow, this place is even better in the daytime than in the night. We should have tried to get some of these bad boys rather than a stinking dagger." She traced the spines of the books like they were gold itself.

Scoffing, I crossed my arms over my chest and leaned against the wall by the door. "Stealing the dagger was a onetime only deal. If you want something, ask for it. Adara would be more than happy to lend it out."

Trisha turned around with a bouncy grin. "That Alec guy was pretty hot. For a serious type anyway. Think he and Adara will do what Octavia said?"

I chuckled. "With Adara's temper? She'd more than likely kill him than fornicate with him."

Wrinkling her nose, Trisha shook her head. "I forget sometimes you're not human. Nobody says fornicate anymore. They say fuck."

I lifted my eyes to the ceiling in silent prayer. "What does it matter what I call it? Either way, they are exchanging bodily fluids. Though, I don't see how it will make them like each other more."

Trisha lifted a shoulder. "Sometimes all that stands between liking and hating someone is a good angry fuck. You'd be surprised how many people only dislike each other because they are fighting their attraction."

"Sounds like you speak from experience."

Blushing slightly, Trisha was saved from answering when Octavia walked into the office.

"Are you ready?" she asked, moving into the room like an otherworldly being and not a fifty-year-old woman.

Shifting away from the wall, I nodded. "Yes, let's get started."

8

"NO. ABSOLUTELY NOT," I quipped, my lip curling in disgust at the cup of putrid liquid Octavia held out to me.

Octavia like many of her kind liked to use herbs. Smelly plants which they set on fire and wave about the room. No idea why they worked. I wasn't God. The small amount of power he bestowed upon mankind was His dirty little secret.

However.

I drew the line at ingesting any of that crap. I was a celestial being, not some human that needed stimulants to open themselves up to other planes of existence.

"I understand your hesitancy, Muriel." Octavia leaned forward in her seat, her eyes way too insightful than I cared for.

I held a hand up, inching away from her in the seat across from her. "Please, Mary. And I don't need that. I don't have a soul to open up to the boundaries of this physical realm."

Octavia smirked. I didn't like that look. It said she knew something I didn't, and I knew everything about myself. Every molecule, every cell, down to the finest hairs on my arm. If I had a soul, I would know. Wouldn't I?

Octavia stared at me, and I stared back determined not to give into her bullying. Finally, after a moment or two, she sighed and withdrew the cup. "Very well have it your way, but if it doesn't work, then will you try?"

Pursing my lips, I narrowed my eyes at her. "Fine. But it will work. Besides, I've already been there before the second time around should be easier right?"

The older woman snorted. "Just because you were in Hell once does not mean you will be able to go back again so easily. We're never the same as we once were. No matter

114

how much we try to pretend. Things change, people change, and you, Mary Wiles, have changed."

I bristled. I had not. I was the same angel I'd always been sans my wings. Sure, I might have blackened my heart some against my superiors, but I hadn't changed that much.

"Stop being stubborn, Mare." Trisha sat down on the arm of my chair. "The more time you waste, the more torture Sid will endure. At this very moment, they could be peeling the skin from his flesh or worse making him watch *Saved By the Bell* reruns." She shuddered visibly.

Sighing my resignation, I held my hand out. "Give me the damn cup."

With a slight tilt of her lips, Octavia handed the cup back to me. I ignored her smug gaze as I downed the horrid concoction. I might not need it to pass between the border of our planes but better safe than sorry. As Trisha said, there was no time to waste.

"You know," Trisha began as I swallow down the disgusting mixture. It tasted like day old burgers and hot garbage all swirled together with a minty finish. "You think you haven't changed, but you have." She grinned down at me and bumped my shoulder. "Remember when you first hired me?"

I smirked. "Yes, you were a foul-mouthed brat who didn't know how to follow orders."

"And you were a self-righteous asswipe who wouldn't dream of cursing. Look at you now."

Rolling my eyes, I handed the cup back to Octavia. "I might have taken on your bad habits, but I'm still -"

"A self-righteous asswipe?"

Shooting Trisha a warning glare, I shoved her off my seat arm. "Still an angel of God."

"Can you really call yourself one of God's angels with your heart full of vengeance?" This question came from Adara who had entered the room without a sound. "Don't try to deny it. We've all seen the anger inside of you. It's the same kind I have for my father."

"And yet you take his place as head of the guild," I countered in return, turning my head to meet her hard gaze.

My eyes followed her as she moved further into the room. She didn't stop at my side where the rest of us gathered but moved behind the large desk. "I became head of the Phoenix Guild for reasons that are my own. I don't have to share them with you."

The harsh tone of her voice surprised me. Adara and I had never had secrets between us. With the way she had talked about the council not being happy with her leadership, I had a feeling it wasn't me that she didn't trust but them. It wasn't safe to talk about it here. Adara would tell me when she was ready.

"So." Trisha cleared her throat. "Now that we've made this as awkward as possible, how about we get this spirit quest underway?" She clapped her hands together and rubbed them, a too eager grin on her face.

I scoffed. "Of course, you're not worried. You're not the one sending their essence to Hell."

Trisha frowned. "Mary, you know that's not what I meant."

I nodded, not meeting her gaze. "I know."

We were all scared. Hell wasn't something to be taken lightly. I should know. I spent enough quality time there. The shadows of my mind threatened to make themselves known, but I pushed them back. I needed my wits about me, not my trauma. I had to keep a clear head so that I could find Sid and Michael's blade. Hopefully, without being discovered myself.

"Octavia?" I glanced over at the psychic who had been watching us with interest. "Are you ready?"

"I only wait for you."

"So, what do I need to do?" I shifted to the end of my chair, my nerves beginning to frazzle. "Will I be able to talk to anyone? Will they be able to see me?"

Shaking her head, Octavia withdrew a small bag. "You will be a ghost on their plane. Able to see and hear but not able to interact. You'll need a portal to be there really."

"And how do we do that?" Trisha asked, sitting down on the ground between us. She crossed her legs and leaned her elbows on her knees. "Do you have something like Michael's blade to open a portal?"

Octavia frowned. "No. I'm afraid I don't have a celestial blade, but we'll come to that once Mary finds what she seeks. No reason to worry about going to Hell unless you have to." The cryptic words she spoke caused the suspicious part of me to rise. Why wouldn't she tell us more about the way into Hell? I was beginning to think she might not be able to get me there like she claimed.

"The next step." Octavia dumped the bag's contents onto the small coffee table between us. Bones. A mixture of rodent and birds' bones. Some of them Octavia had wrapped in twine to form different shapes. Some kind of talismans?

Trisha reached out and picked up one of the bones and twine objects. Octavia didn't stop her, so they must not be something sacred. She turned it over in her hand and even brought it up to her nose to give it a sniff. With a grimace, she dropped it back on the table. "What's all this? Going to summon the spirit of Colonel Sanders to guide Mary into Hell? Because I have to say I'm not surprised, his blend of special seasonings has to be from the devil himself."

"Who's Colonel Sanders?" I asked.

Octavia lifted her eyes to the ceiling, and Adara chuckled my question ignored. Octavia then lifted a hand over the table before us muttering some words in a language I couldn't quite place. The air in the room thickened, killing Adara and Trisha's laughter. The bones on the coffee table twitched and shifted. Suddenly, the separate pieces jumped together into one being. Trisha gasped. Adara moved closer to us her eyes on the bundle of bones and twine. If they were supposed to make some kind of symbol, it wasn't one I was familiar with.

The liquid I had ingested swirled inside of me making me feel like I might vomit at any moment. I fell forward, my hand reaching out to catch me on the coffee table. Octavia lowered her eyes from the ceiling to focus on the bones in front of her. She said a few more words before she locked her eyes on me. "It's time."

The hand pointed at the bones moved from it to hover over me. The feel that overcame me I could only describe as a pulling sort of feeling. Like some unknown force was trying to move me without my permission. It didn't hurt exactly, but it wasn't a pleasant experience. Without warning, the vomiting sensation intensified, and I was dry heaving onto the table. My eyes widened as a white kind of smoke billowed from my mouth.

The more white smoke that came from me, the harder it was to breathe. My mind clouded and my senses dulled. I was on the verge of passing out but not. Then, all of a sudden, it stopped. I could think again, but I was numb. I stared down at my hands and touched each finger to their tips. Nothing.

My eyes turned to Octavia, but she wasn't across from me anymore but to the left. In front of me sat Trisha with Adara standing close behind her. To my right, slouched in my chair sat me. My head hung down between my arms, my shoulders moving up and down as I breathed. So obviously, I was still alive.

"What happened?" Trisha asked, reaching out to touch me.

"Don't. You mustn't," Octavia warned, causing Trisha to drop her hand. "Her essence is no longer in that form. If you disturb her body, she may not be able to find her way back."

"Okay," Adara drew out, her arms crossed over her chest as her eyes scoured the room. "Then where is she?"

"I'm right here," I tried to tell her, but she didn't even acknowledge that she had heard me. I moved closer to them, but none of their eyes pulled to me. I waved a hand in front of Adara's face, but I wasn't there. At least, not to her.

"Mary is now on the spiritual plane," Octavia explained, leaning back in her seat. She didn't seem worried at all that they couldn't see or hear me. "She won't be able to contact us, but we can talk to her."

"Cool." Trisha grinned, her eyes searching the room. "Hey, Mary. If you can hear me give me a sign."

I glanced down at the table and tried to pick up the cup I'd drunk from before. My hand passed right through it. Okay, that didn't work.

"She won't be able to do that," Octavia told Trisha. Too little, too late. "She is a spectator, nothing more." Turning her attention from Trisha, Octavia's eyes seemed to seek me out. They landed on where I stood quite easily. If she couldn't see me, maybe she felt my presence? She was psychic, after all. "Mary, you don't have a lot of time. The spirit can only be away from its body for a certain amount of time before it loses its anchor. You must pass between the barrier of the spiritual plane to Hell."

I placed my hands on my hips or at least tried to. "How do I do that?" My brows furrowed, and I tried to look for some a way to do what she told me.

Thankfully, Trisha was thinking the same question. "How does she do that? Is there a door or maybe a magic word?"

Combing her fingers through her curls, Octavia explained, "She only needs to focus on where she wants to go, and her spirit will take her there. Focus, Mary. You said you've been to Hell before?" I nodded. "Then think of where you want to be, where you have been before and will it so. But do not tarry. You don't want to be stuck there with no way back."

Not feeling any more confident in her instructions than before, I took a deep breath and blew it out. Closing my eyes, I opened my mind to the shadows. I usually fought not to think about my time in Hell.

Darkness surrounded me, a single swinging light bulb hung above my head. Something dripped in the distance. And the laughter. The pain.

Before I even opened my eyes, I knew something had changed. The air around me felt different. Slowly opening my eyes, I found myself no longer in the office, but in the room that I'd been tortured in for days on end. I was in Hell.

9

I COULDN'T SMELL THE air around me, but it definitely didn't feel like Earth anymore. It was heavier like some kind of weight had been added to my shoulders. However, if my senses were working, I would know that the air would be hot and stifling and yet a chill would rush through the body never quite comfortable. The scent of blood and brimstone would burn my nose, and the constant need to vomit would churn around in my stomach.

Snapping out of my stroll down memory lane, I remembered I didn't have long, and I wouldn't find answers in my cell. Moving across the room, I stared at the door. Could

I go through walls? The only way I would know would be to try it.

Bracing myself for pain, I took the few steps toward the door. Blinking in the hallway, I didn't give myself time to find relief in not running into the door before I headed down the hallway. I didn't know where I was going, but I knew one thing. Demons talked. They didn't like anything more than to talk shit about each other. Especially, a half breed. Someone would be talking about Sidney, I just had to find out who.

In Hell, demons didn't have to possess someone to have a physical form which meant they had their own grotesque ones here. Not all of them did. Demons were ultimately fallen angels or humans corrupted by the damning actions that brought them there. The more corrupted they were, the more grotesque they looked. I'm talking horns in strange places, eyes covering every inch of their bodies, and worse yet the stench. Hygiene was not exactly a high priority or any at all.

There were some demons however who enjoyed looking like a human. If they had the powers, they could hide their demon form behind a pretty face, but they would gut you just as fast and smile while doing it.

However, the demons I found weren't high up on the power level. They weren't much more than sniveling bottom feedings. Most of them crawling around on all fours, their arms and legs bent in the wrong direction, their eyes black and mouths full of sharp teeth.

"The boss won't like it." The words came out of the demon's mouth like it had been swallowing glass.

"Then you better find the bastard before he finds out," another demon hissed, shoving the first demon out of the way as they walked, well, more like scurried down the hallway. The walls in here were much different from the ones in my old cell. They looked more like the peeling wallpaper in a haunted house than the cave-like stone of my cell. It made me wonder who exactly thought up this whole freak show. Then again, God created Heaven. It stands to reason he had a hand in Hell.

The demon's conversation was interesting though. Someone had escaped. Would it be too big of a coincidence for it to be someone else other than Sid?

I think not.

To follow the demons or to search out this missing person on my own? Decisions, decisions. When I caught sight of a familiar dark head of hair trying their best to sneak down the hall. Decision made for me, I hurried after Sid, worry eating at me.

If only I could reach out and touch him. Grab his hand and pull him back to Earth with me. But I knew I couldn't I wasn't really there. Not physically anyway.

Following closely behind him, I watched him limp down the hallway. Scurrying feet sounded, and Sid pressed against the wall. It gave me a chance to look him over more clearly. His lip was busted, and bruises bloomed on the left side of his face. Other than being dirty and a bit worse for wear he didn't look like he had been tortured for the last few months. Why was that?

When the demons had hurried passed, Sid began to move once more. He looked like he knew exactly where he was going. He didn't hesitate at any turn or backtrack. The question was where was he going?

We turned once more and found ourselves at a dead end. Sid glanced around before pressing his hand against the side of the wall. The wall gave underneath his hand, opening the wall and exposing a dark room inside. Sid ducked in, pulled a switched that lit the room.

"Wow," I gaped. The room was filled with artifacts that we had been looking for since the fall of Babylon. Sid however ignored all those and went straight for a table at the end of the room. On a stand, sitting in the middle of several other knives sat Michael's dagger.

Sid wrapped his hand around the dagger and lifted it. Holding it tightly in his hand, he turned on his heels only to stop cold. His eyes widened, and surprise covered his face. At first, I thought he could see me, but then the clicking of a tongue made me spin around.

"Well, well, leaving so soon?" Asmodeus, the demon lord himself, stood in the doorway to the secret room. The demon lord had chosen to keep the body he had possessed, some hot shot actor, the poor bastard. It was a bit unnerving to see the burning red eyes in the human face he was wearing. Though, I suppose it was better than the biblical image of him. I could use without seeing if he actually had a horn between his legs. Trisha would be so disappointed in me.

"Get out of my way," Sid growled, holding the dagger in front of him like a weapon. Too bad it wouldn't cut anything without the help of an archangel.

"Now is that any way to treat your father? Especially, after you betrayed me." Asmodeus tapped his chin with his finger. "I could have sent you to the pit but call me sentimental, but I still have high hopes for you."

"Fuck you." Sid spat at Asmodeus's feet. "I'm still a prisoner, and I won't ever come over to your side."

Asmodeus didn't seem at all disheartened by Sid's words. "Flattery will get you everywhere, and I feel like you will be singing a different tune very soon." Asmodeus disappeared from the doorway and reappeared next to side. Sid grunted and folded at the waist as Asmodeus's fist found its home in his gut.

I cried out and tried to jump at Asmodeus but fell straight through him with a frustrated growl.

Plucking the knife from Sid's hand, Asmodeus spun it around in his fingers. "Now, usually I would have scooped your eyes from your head, cut your tongue out, and flayed you alive for a betrayal like you did. But you," - he bent down to meet Sid's eyes - "you are my son. My only son, and if I can't control you, what does that make me?" Asmodeus touched his chest with a sincere question in his eyes.

"An asshole," I quipped. Even though he couldn't hear me, it still made me feel better.

"It makes me look weak, and I can't have that, not with the King breathing down my neck." He snapped his fingers, and two demons appeared. "Take my son back to his room and make sure he stays there."

"Yes, my lord." They hurried into the small room and grabbed at Sid. Sid never to one to make things easy, punch the first one who touched him and then head-butted the other one, sending him spiraling across the room.

Clapping my hands, I laughed. "That's my guy." I had the sudden urge to kiss him and then it was gone as I realized once more that I wasn't here.

"I have to do everything myself." Asmodeus threw his head back and sighed, clearly irritated. As Sid tried to dart for the door, Asmodeus's arm shot out and grabbed him by the back of the neck. Spinning Sid around, he slammed him against the wall. Asmodeus's hand wrapped around the one holding the dagger and pressed until Sid cried out and his fist fell open. The dagger fell to the ground where Asmodeus snatched it up and tucked it into the front of his pants. "I think it's time, dear son of mine, to stop waiting for you to come around and start acting like the demon you are. Whether you like it or not."

Asmodeus grabbed Sid by the front of his shirt and shoved him at the two demons who had recovered from Sid's attack. "Take him back to his room, I'll be there shortly to bring him back to our side." The demons began to take Sid away, but Asmodeus stopped them. "Oh, and the next time he gets away, it will be you who finds their way into the pit." If the demons could have had facial expressions, they would have been quaking in their, well, large hairy feet.

The moment the demons took Sid away I was torn. Did I follow Sid or stay behind with Asmodeus? I knew what I wanted to do. I wanted to follow Sid. To try to find some way to contact him, to get him out of there. However, I knew my time was short and following Sid wouldn't tell me what Asmodeus was planning. And with the mention of the King. I could only assume he meant the King of Hell himself. If he was involved, then I had to find out what they were up to.

Asmodeus stood in the vault-like room for a moment, flipping the dagger over in his hands before taking it back to the table. He placed it on the stand and then left the room. Following after him, I wondered if he could feel my presence. I mean, I was staring daggers into his back. I really wished I was there right then. With my gun in my hand, so I could put a holy bullet in Asmodeus's smug face.

The further into the depths of Hell we went, the more I felt the weight pushing down on me. Something in my chest told me to not go any further to go back the way I came but I couldn't, not yet. I still had time, I needed to find out what they were planning, and Asmodeus was the only lead I had.

We rounded one more corner and then entered a large room. Like some scene out of one of those movies Trisha made me watch, a large chair sat at the top of a long black-topped table. Asmodeus withdrew the dagger and sat it on top of the table. Sighing, he leaned his hands against the top of the table.

"Oh, poor demon lord," I mock pouted behind his back. "Stressed out by your rebellious son. If only there were someone who could help you, who knew how you felt. Oh wait, that would be God, but you already burned that bridge, now didn't you?"

"You're late," a smooth voice rippled through the room. Asmodeus's head jerked up and searched the room before landing on the high-back chair where a handsome blonde man sat. He wore a suit and had an impatient frown on his lips.

"My apologies." Asmodeus straightened up, adjusting his clothing before approaching the man. I didn't need to ask who he was. I hadn't seen him in centuries but even if I didn't know him the tremble that rushed through Asmodeus at the very presence of the man before him would have tipped me off.

Samael. The Bright Morning Star and a huge pain in my and every other angels' ass in Heaven. Lucifer, the King of Hell.

"What are you doing with Asmodeus?" I mused aloud. My breath caught as Lucifer's face jerked to the side, his eyes locking on where I stood. Could he see me?

10

IN HEAVEN, IT WASN'T like everyone knew everyone. There were the higher up angels — called the archangels — which everyone knew. Believe me, sometimes the cons far outweighed the pros.

Sure, I could get just about anyone to do anything I wanted but I also couldn't go where I wanted without people hounding me at every moment. My movements were watched every moment of every minute of my existence. Trisha would call me one of the Kardashians of Heaven. She wasn't wrong.

But even though we were all archangels, there were various levels of that as well. I would have been the lowest you could be. Still famous, still prayed to by the churches, not like that ever achieved anything. Angels, unless they have fallen weren't allowed to do much more than watch. Not unless God allowed it. Ramiel had been my commander. He trained me, gave me orders from God, and kept my confidence. Until he too betrayed Heaven... and me.

It made me wonder if he had been in contact with Lucifer, after all. The angel with a plan, the reason why all angels were forbidden to go against God unless they want to suffer the same fate as him. A right dick.

Lucifer had the ear of God. He was his favorite son. However, he had taken that favoritism too far. Lashing out against the humans, God's favorite of his creations, and had found himself falling. It had Heaven in an uproar for centuries. If Lucifer, God's chosen, was not safe from banishment than none of us were.

There had been a few who had fallen with him, choosing exile over following God any longer, just waiting for the day that they fucked up.

None of them realized how little God actually cared for us. I'd messed up. Gone against orders and I had not been cast out. He hadn't helped me exactly either. It was a question I'd asked myself nightly for the first few years on Earth. However, I could never test that theory because I didn't have my wings. Still couldn't.

But if Lucifer was involved in anything, then I knew it had to be trouble.

"Are we alone?" Lucifer asked, his eyes still boring into the spot where I stood, too petrified of being caught to move. Lucifer was a right bastard himself. I'd never been afraid of him, and he had his head shoved too far up his own ass to bother with me. Didn't keep me from being cautious.

"Of course, my king." Asmodeus brought a fist to his chest and bowed his head slightly.

Lucifer stood from his chair and moved away from the table. Walking toward me, I stayed as still as possible. Lucifer walked straight through me and to the door. Jerking it open, two scared shitless demons fell into the doorway. They gaped up at Lucifer and began to grovel.

Scowling as if he couldn't be bothered, he flicked his wrist. The two demons before him howled in agony before they melted into the floor. Ducking a head out the door, he then closed it with a resounding snap before turning back to the Asmodeus. "You must work on your security, Asmodeus."

"My apologies, my king. This is a stressful time for all of us." Lucifer gave Asmodeus a burning glare. "Of course, that is no excuse for laziness. I will make sure our security is more diligent." Asmodeus moved toward the door, but Lucifer held a hand up. "My king?"

"Later. We are short on time, and there are things to discuss."

Lucifer strode across the room before gracefully taking his seat once more. Good to see some things never change. For all his faults, Lucifer had always been one for looks and how one presents themselves. The suit he wore didn't belong in Hell, but no doubt he has been waiting to go to Earth and this appearance was in preparation for that moment.

"Now, I know it took me a while to come to visit you, but things in the inner circle are far more tremulous than you would believe. The other lords want blood. They want carnage, and they want to know what is taking so damn long." Lucifer slammed his hands on the top of the table making Asmodeus and myself jump. At least, I wasn't the only one who was a bit jumpy.

A part of me felt good to see Asmodeus quake before the King of Hell. He had caused so much pain and suffering already it was only fair for him to have his own shoved upon him. And I knew Lucifer would love nothing better than to tear the demon lord's head from his shoulders and use his skull as a nut cup.

Lucifer might play the part of the doting king to his loyal - more like terrified into submission - subjects, but if everyone thought Lucifer hated humans above all else, they would be wrong. No, that special spot was reserved for demons, the filth of the human and angel race. Something Lucifer abhorred more than anything, imperfection.

"My king." Asmodeus dropped to his knees beside Lucifer his hands clasped in front of him. "I am but your humble servant. I do not have the powers to make events unfold the way we wish it. Not like you our tremendous benevolent king."

"Stop with the groveling, Asmodeus. It is not becoming." Lucifer sighed and rubbed his temples. "Did you get the dagger or not?"

Asmodeus jumped to his feet, nodding eagerly. "Yes, yes we did."

Lucifer held his hands open and stared at the demon lord. "Well, where is it?"

With a grimace, Asmodeus took a step back from the King of Hell. "It is somewhere safe. We have run into a few complications that require the blade to be kept out of sight."

"What kind of complications?"

"Well, my son for one."

Lucifer's lips pinched into a brilliant smile. The only sign he was upset the twitch by his left eye. A telltale sign that Ramiel had pointed out to me back in Heaven. "Your son?"

"Yes, my king." Asmodeus ducked his head, he too had figured out the mask of the archangel.

"The same son who came from the human whore you defiled?" his voice raised as he stood from his chair once more, Asmodeus shaking in his boots before him. "The same son I told you to destroy in his very crib? That son?"

"My king, I have gone against your wishes, yes, but it is fortuitous for us today." Asmodeus held his hands up in surrender to enraged being before him. "My son has become a powerful demon—"

"Half demon."

"Yes, but a powerful one and has gained the looks of his mother making him quite the tool to be used against the humans."

"What do I care for them? I only care about my plans. Plans I thought you understood." Lucifer's arm shot out and his fingers wrapped around Asmodeus's neck. Lifting the demon up in the air, Lucifer snarled at him. "You could ruin the plan I'd been working on since before my fall from Heaven. Tell me your sentimentality for your son did not ruin it?"

Asmodeus gasped and grabbed at Lucifer's fingers, his eyes bulging from his head. Lucifer loosened his grasp so that the squirming demon could talk. "My son is bait."

"Bait? Why would we need bait?" Lucifer scowled, his fingers tightening around his throat once more.

Asmodeus's legs kicked and tried to talk a few times but then could only get one word out. A name. My name.

"Muriel?" Lucifer arched a perfect eyebrow. "What of her?"

Pointing a finger at his throat, Asmodeus tried to talk once more. With a reluctant sigh, Lucifer dropped the demon letting him fall to the floor in a heap. Pulling in hard lungfuls of air, Asmodeus looked up to his king. "She's on Earth. Fallen like you."

"No, I'm not," I growled though none of them could hear me. "I'm not fallen. You stole my wings, you boot licking asswipe!" I marched over to Asmodeus and kicked at him. Of course, my foot went straight through him which only made me kick harder.

Lucifer chuckled, making me stop my attack. "The pure and precious Muriel has fallen? How... quaint. And what does that have to do with anything? She can't use the dagger if she's fallen."

Asmodeus finally got his feet back under him and grinned. "Maybe fallen is not the right word."

"Then what would be?" Asmodeus started to speak, but Lucifer held up his hand. "I'm losing my patience if the next words out of your mouth are not what I want to hear I will make you clean the pit until that meat suit you are wearing peels from your body."

A flicker of panic filled Asmodeus's eyes, and he nodded. "We clipped her wings. We have them. Here. She's still an angel. An archangel."

I started forward at the mention of my wings but then stopped at the look on Lucifer's face. What was he thinking?

Lucifer stared at him for a moment and then threw his head back and laughed. The sound of it raced over my form and made me shudder. It reverberated off the walls and even the rock beneath crumbled at its sound. When he was done laughing, Lucifer smirked, stroking a finger over his cheek. "An archangel without her wings. Oh, she must be hating that."

"Not so much." Asmodeus shrugged. "She has taken up the name Mary Wiles and has been playing detective and demon hunter on Earth." Asmodeus paused, hesitating to say the last part. "And... taken my son as her lover."

"Oh, now that is too wonderful." Lucifer clasped his hands together in front of his face, pressing his lips to the sides of them. "So, you are telling me we have Michael's blade, Muriel's wings, and her lover?"

"Yes, and I have my spies on Earth watching her every move. She is desperately trying to find a way back into Hell." Asmodeus smiled largely, and I couldn't help but put my fist through his face and wiggle it around. It didn't do anything, but it sure made me feel better.

"This is perfect." Lucifer paced in front of us. "We can use the lover and her wings as leverage to get her to use Michael's blade for me."

"That would be a fuck you." I spat on the floor before him. "I won't do anything for you."

"Tell me." Lucifer adjusted his cufflinks. "How does she look? Still as radiant as ever?"

Asmodeus nodded, eagerly. I grimaced at the lust in his eyes. "She's a nice piece even as a human. I almost had a taste, and I can tell you it was-"

Lucifer's hand threw out all of a sudden knocking Asmodeus into the other wall. "You dare touch one of mine?"

"But my king, she's the enemy." Asmodeus fell to his knees before Lucifer.

"Enemy or not, she's still one of mine. If anyone would taste her human flesh, it will be me." Lucifer scowled at Asmodeus, and then a secret grin curled up his lips. "Once she opens the way to Heaven, and I take back what is rightfully mine, she'll stand at my side. So, tell me how we are going to get her here?"

"Fat chance, you inflated daddy's boy," I snarled but then stopped. I felt strange. Different. My eyes searched the room for what had changed and realized I couldn't hear Asmodeus's reply to Lucifer. I rushed over to his side and arched my body next to his trying to make out his words.

Nothing. I couldn't hear anything. What was going on?

In my panic the world around me became fuzzy. The walls seemed like they were melting right before my eyes and I rushed to stop it. I wasn't done. I needed more time.

"No, no," I shouted as the world around me faded, and the office in the Phoenix Guild mansion began to reappear. Trisha's worried face pushed into mine, her hands grabbing the sides of my face. When my eyes fluttered open, she sighed in relief.

"Finally! Shit, Mary, you scared the life out of me."

"What?" I shook my head, staring around the room without really seeing it. "What's going on? Where am I?"

"You're back."

11

I JERKED OUT OF Trisha's grasp and jumped out of my chair. Irritation filled me as I paced the floor. Lucifer had been in on it this whole time. How had I not seen that? Of course, that snobby egotistical ass would be in on it.

I scoffed and shook my head.

"Mary, what is it?" Adara asked coming close to me but not touching me. "What did you see?"

I paused my pacing to look at them. Trisha had her hands clasped together in front of her, her eyes pinched with worry.

Adara had her hands on her hips, her shoulders bunched up to her ears. Octavia was the only one who didn't seem too worried about what I had seen.

My eyebrows bunched as my jaw clenched. "Did you know? Did you know what they had planned?"

"Now, hold up." Trisha moved over to stand by Octavia, she placed a defensive hand on her shoulder. "What does Octavia have to do with anything?"

Octavia patted Trisha's hand to try to placate her and then turned her body toward me. "I did not know what they planned, but I have heard trickles of rumors. Things that may or may not be planned." She shrugged. "One does not believe everything that they hear lest they be a fool."

"Still," I bit out, taking a step toward her, "a little warning would have been nice."

"I did not know what you would or wouldn't hear. Why worry you for needless reasons?" Octavia shook her head and pinched her lips together. "I haven't lived this long by giving away all that I see. Else, I would have been on the guild's radar far sooner than now."

"Believe me, we won't make that same mistake again," Adara quipped, her expression nothing short of lethal.

Octavia was not endearing herself to any of us with keeping secrets. Well, maybe Trisha. She still didn't see the error of Octavia's omission. If she knew what I would be walking into she should have told me from the get-go, not let me go in blind.

"Can someone tell me what's going on in words I'll understand?" Trisha threw her hands up in agitation. "I really hate when you talk around me."

Forcing my eyes away from Octavia, I turned to my assistant. Jaw still clenched, I tried my best not to yell. "What Octavia has failed to do alert us of, is that Asmodeus isn't working alone. It's not his plan at all, actually."

"Wait a second." Trisha held a hand up. "Then who's plan was it to steal Michael's dagger and take over the world?"

"Who fucking else?" I practically screamed unable to hold back my anger any longer. "The oh-I'm-so-much-greater-than-any-of-you Lucifer." My fingers curled into fists, and I had the sudden urge to punch something. I settled for pacing some more.

"You mean, the Lucifer? The actual devil?" Trisha gaped at me. There were fear and a hint of excitement in her words. I wasn't surprised by how she reacted to me being an angel. Of course, she would be all fangirling over the dark lord himself. I snorted. Dark Lord, my holy ass. More like compensating for a small dick.

"Don't go wetting your pants over him," Adara interjected with a warning look. "He's not all that a bag of chips. Believe me, I've heard of his antics. They usually end up with a body count of astronomical sizes."

Trisha frowned, her excitement deflating slightly but only slightly. "But what does he had to do with any of this? He's the one who wanted us to steal the dagger?"

I dragged a hand over my face and shook my head. "No, I think that was all Asmodeus, but Lucifer did want Michael's blade. He didn't even know I was here on Earth let alone that I had been captured and tortured there."

Trisha let out an unbelieving laugh. "How can the ruler of Hell not know who's being tortured there?"

I gave her a sideways look. "He's not God. He's not all knowing. Lucifer might want everyone to think he knows everything, but he's not much more powerful than Ramiel or me. He's simply done a good job building up his reputation."

"You mean, he wasn't much more powerful than you," Adara reminded me with a point of her finger.

"What's that supposed to mean?"

"Well, in Heaven, you had your wings and all your holy powers. You would be as powerful as Lucifer if not more with him being fallen. But now that you are on Earth without your wings as well and having used up quite a bit of your holy abilities recently, you probably shouldn't be going toe to toe with him any time soon. At least, not on your own."

I stared at her for a moment. Damn. She was right. I hated to admit it, but she was. I wasn't anywhere near Lucifer's level of power the way I was now. Maybe if I had my wings, but that was a whole other issue altogether.

"I need my wings back." I rubbed my chin and glared at the ground. "If I had them, then I could beam Lucifer's lily-white ass back to the pit where he belonged."

Trisha frowned at me, moving away from Octavia to stand by my side. "But you don't have them or even know where they are."

I stopped pacing, and a slow grin spread across my face. "Oh, yes I do. One of the things I heard in Hell was that very tidbit. Asmodeus has them."

"He does?"

"How'd that happen?"

I waved off their questions. "The how isn't important the why is. He thinks he can use them and Sid as bait to get me to use the dagger for them."

"But you're not going to fall for it right?" Trisha wrung her hands together, worry making her forehead bunch together.

I sighed. "What choice do I have? It's a lose/lose situation. I have to get my wings to be able to beat Lucifer and stop his plan for world domination and conquering Heaven, or we're all doomed."

"But they are expecting you to come for your wings," Adara argued. "You're walking right into a trap."

I lifted a shoulder but didn't argue. It was a trap. Lucifer and Asmodeus had said as much, but I didn't have another choice. "Do you have a better idea? I'm not leaving Sid there regardless of if I get my wings back or not."

"You care for this man quite a lot I gather." Octavia's voice caused me to jump in place. I had forgotten she was there.

I stared her down, wondering where she was going with her statement. "Yes, I do."

"Then you would do anything to get him back?"

I nodded my head. "I'm walking into a trap just to save him. I think that pretty much sums it up."

"Good." Octavia used her can to stand up. Trisha rushed to her side to help her to her feet. "I wasn't sure you would be able to handle what will be required of you to get into Hell, but after hearing your squabbles, I know now that you are ready."

"Ready for what?" Adara asked, suspicion in her voice.

"For Mary to go to Hell, she will have to do something that is against her nature. It will hurt quite a bit." Octavia locked eyes with me, seriousness filling her face. "You won't like it, and your body will fight it. It might even taint your angelic aura."

I didn't like the sound of that, but there wasn't much else I could do. Without Michael's blade, I had no way into Hell. Not unless I found another portal which the demons were not being very open about where those were located. Octavia was my only chance at getting into Hell and getting Sid and my wings back. Whatever she thought I needed to do I had to do it. Regardless of if I would like it or not. Besides, how bad could it be?

"Alright." I took a deep breath and let it out. "What do I need to do?"

"You can't be serious," Adara cried out, grabbing my shoulder. "You don't know what this ritual might do to you. You should let me make some inquiries first."

"We don't have time for that," I reminded her. "The ritual has to be done on a full

155

moon. That's not long from now. Do you think you could get all the information you need before then?"

Adara pursed her lips. "Possibly but still you shouldn't go into this blind."

"I'm not. I already got a peek at what I'm getting into. I even know where they are holding Michael's blade and Sid, so I won't be walking in there all willy-nilly."

"Willy-nilly." Trisha giggled.

Rolling my eyes at her, I turned back to Octavia. "While Adara is finding more out about your ritual, you tell me what I need to do to prepare."

"First," she started in a cryptic tone, "you will need a demon."

12

FINDING A DEMON WOULD be easy enough but the rest of the things Octavia asked for Adara had to find. I wouldn't even know where to get half the crap she asked for. Who had the bones of a three-day-old calf just lying around? Whatever, that was Adara's problem, not mine. I had enough on my own plate to worry about. Starting with finding this missing boy.

"So, you're going to fly to Seattle find the guy and fly back?" Trisha asked as she packed my clothes into a duffel bag. I didn't travel often, if at all, so I didn't own any fancy suitcases, duffel bags were as fancy as I got.

"Yep." I checked that my back-up gun was filled with holy bullets and shoved a few more clips into my duffel. I couldn't carry them on me because of the plane, and it pains me to not have my gun on me but when playing human one had to play by the human rules. For the most part.

"And you don't think you need any help? Like maybe back up?"

I knew what she was getting at, but I wasn't going to ask Adara to come with me. I needed her here finding out more about the ritual Octavia wanted to perform. Also, it was a good idea to keep Adara away from as many vampires as possible. She hadn't told me much about any vampire lovers recently, but it was better not to tempt her. The last thing I needed was to be fighting and have her jump sides.

"No," I said to Trisha leaving out all the things I wanted to say. "It'll be fine. It's only a nest of vamps, nothing I can't handle."

"But you are still recovering from the thing with Asmodeus and Ramiel. Have you even fought more than one demon at a time lately?"

I didn't like the tone of her voice. Like she didn't believe I could take care of myself. Had I really gotten so bad that my own assistant had to worry about me?

"I'll be fine. I promise I won't do anything rash. Okay?"

Trisha frowned. "Fine. But if you die. I'm going to kick your ass."

I laughed harder than I should have. Trisha gave me a curious look, making me stop short. "It's fine, Trisha. I mean it. I'll be fine."

"You said fine way too many times. I'm starting to think you don't even think you'll be fine." Trisha crossed her arms over her chest and tapped her foot. "At least, ask Thompson to help you out."

"Can't." I shook my head, zipping my bag up and pulling it over my shoulder. "He's busy with his own demon."

"Which is all the more reason to stay here." She dashed in front of me, blocking my exit. "Help Thompson with his demon, and he can help you with yours."

"Pfft." I ducked my head and blew out a breath. "Why the need to keep me here all the sudden? I thought you were all hung up me getting money to keep this place running?"

Trisha dropped her arms. "That was before I knew the King of Hell wanted you to help him take over the world. Now, keeping the lights on seems kind of trivial." She lifted her hands and flopped them back down.

I dropped my bag onto the floor and wrapped my arms around Trisha, pulling her into a hug. I didn't do physical comfort often. I didn't really see the point, but Trisha was young and human. She still needed to be coddled when she was worried.

I stroked her hair and made a cooing noise in the back of my throat. "Don't worry Trisha. Everything will be okay. I promise you."

Trisha sniffled and buried her face in my neck. "I just don't want to lose my best friend."

"You won't." I pulled back and smiled down at her. "At least, not until we find this guy. Then it's up in the air. Though, I'm pretty sure I can handle whatever Lucifer plans to throw at me."

"What if he has legions of demons waiting for you?" she rubbed her hand across her nose and eyes smearing her makeup. "What if this whole thing goes to hell - no pun intended - and you end up back in that cell? I don't want you to be tortured!"

"I don't either." I placed my hands on her shoulders and squeezed lightly. "But if I don't go and stop them, then Sid could be the one getting tortured, and they could find another archangel they can force to use Michael's blade. At least if I go, then we know I won't do what they want."

Trisha heaved a heavy sigh. "Fine. You can go but you better not get sidetracked. You find the boy and get him back to his parents." She paused and made a face. "You know, if he is alive, but don't be a hero. Don't take on more than you can handle. And call! Every hour."

I arched a brow.

"Okay, every few hours. Just to check in and make sure you're not getting in over your head."

"Is this like in those movies where I call you my mother with a teasing connotation?" I cocked my head to the side with a wry grin.

Trisha puffed up and then shuddered. "Don't call me that. I'd rather be dead than my mother."

I laughed and grabbed my bag, throwing an arm around her shoulders as I walked toward the front door. "I think you should get your priorities straight."

"My priorities are straight. No one wants to be compared to their mother. Least of all me." she pointed a finger at her chest and then moved out from under my arm, walking backward toward the door. "You would hate it if I compared you to Ramiel wouldn't you?"

I scowled. "First of all, that's not the same thing. Ramiel was my commander, not my mother. I don't have a mother. I have a father who has more of a let the older siblings handle the bulk of the teaching and commanding than anything else. I've never even met him, and I'm an archangel." I pushed past her and bounded down the stairs.

"How's that even possible?" Trisha hurried after me, calling over my shoulder. "You both lived in Heaven. You're one of his favorite's chosen ones. Daddy dearest never came by to even say hi?"

"No."

"Not even on your birthday?"

I glanced over my shoulder at her. "I don't have a birthday, and you forget I'm an angel, not a human. We don't do emotion well let alone the sentimentality of recognizing one's day of birth."

"I guess so," Trisha trailed off and then giggled. "If you did have a birthday, I bet you'd hate it, anyway."

"Why's that?" I pushed the lower door open and stepped out into the night air. Lou's was working hard with the sound of customers coming in and out of the doors. It was dinner time, so it wasn't unusual and simply hearing the restaurant's bustle made me hungry. Damn human condition.

Trisha stepped out of the building and stopped at my side. "I mean that if you did have a birthday, you would have to share it with like a billion other angels, so it wouldn't be all that fun in the first place."

I pursed my lips. "I can see what you mean. However, there are not billions of angels in Heaven."

"There's not?"

"More like trillions. I don't have a recent headcount though. I have been out of the loop lately." I gave her a meaningful look before heading toward her car. "Are you sure it's okay for you to drop me off? I can drive myself, I still have Sid's truck."

"No way and pay the parking fee?"

I rolled my eyes. Throwing my bag into the back of the car, I climbed into the passage side. Trisha entered the driver's side and cranked the car, her radio coming on blaring some heavy rock music. "So, did you call Thompson and get some information about the missing kid?"

"Uh, yeah. I messaged him about it. He's supposed to have called the local police. They're supposed to give me all the details when I get there."

"That's a lot of supposeds. Are you anticipating trouble?"

"When am I not?" I shifted in the driver seat and turned down the radio. Trisha might like her eardrums to bleed, but I needed every sense I had if I was going up against Lucifer. "I'm not exactly expecting a warm welcome, but most police officers don't want outside people poking around in their business. I'd be lucky to get a missing person's report from them."

"Ah, yeah, that doesn't sound promising."

We drove the rest of the way to the airport in near-silence. Every once in a while, Trisha would make a comment, but I wasn't much in the talking mood. My mind had too much going around in it. There was the missing boy, the demon killer, and now Lucifer of all things. My plate was pretty full, and it didn't look like it would lighten up anytime soon.

"Okay, you're all set." Trisha turned in her seat. "You have your ID, right? And your ticket?"

"Yes, both."

"And don't forget they make you go through a metal detector, so you have to take your shoes off, and you don't have any weird anomalies that could be picked up by an x-ray, right? Or those drug-sniffing dogs?"

I smirked. "No, it'll be fine. I have gone through this before."

"Alright, alright. I'm sorry. I don't mean to nag, but I don't want anything to happen to you. We still need you to save the world here."

"But only after I make a paycheck," I teased and patted her hand. "Everything will be great. You hold down the fort. Maybe check on Octavia see if she needs anything or maybe some company."

"You mean spy on her and make sure she's who she says she is and not working for the Dark Lord."

"That's my good little secretary." I pinched her cheek, and she jerked away from me rubbing it.

"Yeah, yeah. Whatever. You don't pay me enough for this crap. Get out of here before I change my mind."

13

THE PLANE TRIP WAS boring. Nothing unexpected happened, and I was able to check into my hotel without any issues. I only hoped the rest of the trip was that uneventful.

The police had already emailed me the file they had on Henry's disappearance which wasn't much at all. I was pretty much starting from scratch, which was at the club Banquet de Rouge.

Unpacking my bag, I found an outfit that Trisha had put in. Leather pants and a dark purple corset. She had argued it would help me blend in better at the vampire club, but I didn't really think a change of clothing would help. Demons had a way of sniffing me out. Vampire or not.

Well, I didn't have anything else to do. I might as well check the club out now. It would give me a clear picture of what I'm up against at least. If I was lucky, I'd close the case tonight and be on my way home tomorrow and a step closer to getting into Hell.

Changing my clothes, I took a moment to look at myself. The pants weren't so constricting that I couldn't move, but the corset top forced my boobs to my chin. Or close enough to it. I left my hair down; my neck was already bare enough I didn't need to give them any ideas of taking a nip at me.

I left my guns in the room because quite frankly I didn't have anywhere to put them that wasn't out in the open. I did slip a small silver dagger with its sheath into my cleavage. The only place that wouldn't be seen. My cellphone went into my back pocket along with my ID. It was all I was getting into these pants.

It was strange. Tonight was different from my usual hunts. I was trying to be subtle, which was usually not my style. I was more of a go in guns blazing with an arsenal big enough for a small army. Only going in with my own powers and a tiny dagger made me feel naked.

Sighing, I grabbed my cell and keys to the rental car before heading out the door. Just as I hit my car, my phone rang. "Hello?"

"Hey, did you land alright? Was there any trouble?" Trisha's worried voice filled the other side of the phone line. I could practically see her shaking through the phone, tying her hair all up in knots from her anxiety.

"Jeez, Trisha. You'd think I was going to Hell or something." I chuckled, getting into the car.

"Not. Funny."

"Everything went as planned. No need to get your panties in a twist. I'm heading over to the club now to scope out the place."

"Are you wearing that outfit I picked?"

"Yes, unfortunately, I am." I shifted uncomfortably as the spines of the corset poked me. "I don't understand how this will help me fit in."

169

Trisha sighed an irritable sigh. "You've been on Earth for how long now? When are you going to learn that down here looks are everything? You can't go to a vamp lair dressed like... well, you. They'll see through it right away."

"And not my angelic aura?" I reminded her.

Sniffing loudly, Trisha huffed. "With that outfit, they won't notice your aura until they are too close to do anything about it. Besides, you're more human than angel right now with your powers not fully charged right?"

I hated that she was right. It's been months, and still, my powers weren't back up to snuff. Sure, I was better than the day after I had let loose my powers on Ramiel, but it still wasn't like before. I'd be lucky to be able to exorcize any demons without my gun or talisman - which the latter I had tucked into my pocket - what little room there was. I only hoped I wouldn't need it or the knife in my cleavage tonight.

"Well, in any case, at least you'll look hot," Trisha squealed and then sighed dramatically into the phone. "I wish I could go."

170

"Yeah, well I'd have felt better with you by my side, but someone needs to keep care of things there. Besides, I don't want your mother coming by to whack me one because I put you in harm's way."

"What harm?"

I snorted. "This coming from the girl who was worried about me going into a nest of vampires on my own."

"Fine. Fine. Have it your way, but still, a vampire club is worth the risk. When am I ever going to get to go to one of them?"

I shook my head at how excited she sounded. "Remind me to take you to the one in LA then we can talk."

"There's one here?" her voice went up a few octaves, making me wince.

"Yes, and don't go looking for them. I promise to take you after this whole mess is over with. Maybe even Adara can come. We both know she knows her way around a vampire or two."

Trisha giggled. "Oh, I'm sure she does."

"I'll call you before I go to bed. Alright?"

"Sounds good. Be careful."

"I will." I hung up the phone and focused on driving. Banquet de Rouge wasn't too far from my hotel which was a good and a bad thing. Not too far meaning it's in a bad area which also meant my hotel was smack dab in the middle of it. I made sure to put all my valuables in the safe provided by the hotel, but even then, I wasn't sure if they were safe. Not that I had many valuables, but my gun and ammo weren't things I wanted to lose in case I needed them.

Since it was after ten o'clock, the club was in full swing and finding a parking spot was ridiculous. By the time I found one, there was a long line around the corner with a large bouncer at the front of it. Loud music came blaring out of the brick building whenever they opened it to let someone inside. I stood at the back of the line for a few moments, irritated at having to wait. I could have bullied my way in but then again, I was trying to blend not draw attention to myself. So, I waited in the line for a good half hour with the humans who were already mostly drunk, and they hadn't even entered the club yet.

Most of them were dressed the same as me if not more extravagant. Trisha would have definitely fit in with this crowd. There

172

was enough eyeliner on their faces to fill a whole pencil and then some. I'd never felt more out of place, and it showed.

"Hey, baby!" A drunken guy waiting next to me tried to cage me in between his arms. "What's a good girl like you doing in a place like this?"

His breath stunk of beer, and I could feel his penis against my hip. Already in a bad mood by the wait, my hand shot out and grabbed him by the testicles he so loved to rub against me and squeezed ever so slightly. "Don't scream. Don't even talk. Just listen."

The guy gasped and then bit his lip, nodding his head rapidly.

"No one here wants to copulate with you. No one wants to feel your microdick on their hip. Least of all me. I'm not here to play around. I'm working. Do you understand?" When he didn't answer, I gave his testicles a bit of pressure. "What was that?"

"Yes, yes. Please god yes. I won't bother you."

"Good." I released him and shoved him away. "Now get out of my sight."

The guy hurried away not even bothering to go into the club even though it was our turn to go up to the large bouncer. A bit happier to be there, I sauntered up to him. The man didn't pretend that he wasn't looking me over, so I didn't either. He had a head the size of a bowling ball which shined as much as one under the street light. His eyes were small and close together. The sweat on his brow dripped into his shirt that covered his massive form. He sat on a bar stool that might collapse at any moment under his weight. The clipboard in his hand seemed to have a list of some kind.

"What's your name, sweetheart?" he grinned at me flashing a silver tooth on either side, the lust in his eyes apparent.

I reached out a hand and touched his, not allowing him to look at his little piece of paper. "I'm whoever you want me to be."

I know it was silly, but I saw it on a movie with Trisha, and I had to try it out. I wasn't on that list, and the only way I was going to get in is either by force or by using the outfit Trisha had picked out. If it didn't work, I was always happy to cause some carnage.

The bouncer chuckled deeply, licking his lips in appreciation. He jerked his head toward the door. "Go on in, love. But come find me later, okay? I'll show you a good time."

"Can't wait," I breathed, batting my eyelashes while inside doing a victory dance.

The music inside the club was even louder than the bits I heard from outside, the air hot and slightly smelling of body odor. I honestly preferred the sidewalk, but I didn't have much of a choice in the matter. I needed Intel, and this was the last place that Henry had been seen at before he was reported missing.

I made my way through the crowd of bodies, pushing hands away from me as they tried to grab at my hips and convince me to dance with them. One got a bit too aggressive and received a good sucker punch for his troubles. By the time I arrived at the bar, I was more than ready for a drink.

"What can I get you?" A woman wearing a corset similar to mine with black hair and tattoos covering her arms and neck. She seemed normal enough, and I couldn't scent any demon inside of her. One quick flick of the veil and I saw she was human. Not a single trace of vampire. "Hello? I don't have all day."

175

"Sorry." I flicked the veil back into place and took the vacated seat in front of me. "I'll have... whatever's good here."

The bartender cocked her brow. "Don't get out much?"

I shook my head and offered a shy smile. Let her think what she wants. "Is it that obvious?"

Smiling slightly, the bartender began to mix a few things into a glass. "No, I've just seen it all. Your type is pretty easy to spot."

"My type, huh?"

"Yeah, the kind who spend most of their days behind a desk or at home with their cats but inside they are longing to find something better. More exciting." She smirked and sat a glass in front of me. The liquid inside was a reddish blue, and when I sniffed it, there wasn't a hint of alcohol. "Don't worry, it won't bite."

I picked up the glass and toasted her silently before taking a sip. A rush of flavors hit my tongue. There was alcohol, but I could barely taste it. It was more of a burn that only added to the robust fruity flavor. "It's really good."

176

"Thanks. I call it the Bloody Angel."

The drink caught in my throat and went down the wrong pipe causing me to beat my chest and cough. "The what?"

"Are you okay?" I waved her off. "It's called the Bloody Angel. I made it one night when I was trying to get over this guy I'd been dating. A real jerkwad if I ever saw one." We exchanged a chuckle. "Anyway, he's one of those guys that has the face of an angel, and I wondered what it would look like all bloody and beaten to a pulp." I stared at her for a moment, and she quickly added, "I was in a really dark place, but this baby came out of it, so it wasn't for nothing, right?"

I smiled tightly. "No, it's great. A real crowd pleaser."

"So glad you like it. Now, keep an eye on your drink and if you need an out, be sure to order a shot of white angel and I'll call the cops. 'K?"

I nodded, and she went back to taking orders. I didn't know exactly what she was talking about, but my last experience with drinking at a place like this had me more than a little cautious to leave my drink with strangers. Angel or not, being roofied was not a pleasant experience.

I turned away from the bar and scanned the room. It was much like any other club I'd been too except the clientele wore more eyeliner and leather than the normal person. The music was right up there with Trisha's kind. Loud and grating. Give me a good old string harp any day.

God, I was lame.

Sadly, no one from the crowd shouted vampire from the look of them. The dim lighting and the thick crowd made it almost impossible to place any faces or get much of a read on the place. I tried to lower the veil on my powers and get a good look, but nothing stood out.

With a dismal sigh, I sat my finished glass on the bar top and abandoned my post. My legs wobbled beneath me, and I shook my head trying to clear it. That drink must have had more alcohol than I thought. The bartender shouted at me, and I waved her off, making my way into the crowd. I just needed to burn some of the alcohol off then when I could finally think I could search for Henry.

I found myself on the dance floor, and I let the music -though grinding - take control. The rapid beat was just the thing I needed to get my blood pumping and the toxins moving through my system. A pair of hands slid onto my hips and a hard front pressed against my back. I started to turn around and shove him away, but they held me with inhuman strength.

"Now, now, pretty little angel. We wouldn't want to cause a scene, now would we?" The words burned into my ear, and I tensed.

I searched around me, my head a bit clearer now, for any other demons. None immediately showed themselves, only the man holding me tight enough to bruise. "What do you want?"

The man laughed, the sound of it made me want to shiver, but I forced it back. "Isn't that my line? You're the one who came into my club, not the other way around."

Before I had a chance to answer, he spun me around so that we were facing each other. The body the demon was possessing - and it was a demon, vampires had a different sort of feel to them - was handsome enough with a head of curly brown hair and a chiseled

179

jawline. His eyes were a deep chocolate brown with a promise of pain mixed with laughter. It was the kind of look that would cause any smart woman to run away as fast as they could. Unfortunately, I wasn't that kind of woman. I had a job to do, and this demon would do it.

"I'm looking for a boy," I told him finally, my hands on his biceps as we pretended to still be dancing.

"Are you sure?" he quirked a brow. "I would have sworn you were looking for a demon."

My lip lifted on one side. "That too, but right now, I'll settle for a boy. Just turned twenty, brown hair, freckles, and goes by the name of Henry Barnes. Seen him?"

"Maybe." The demon's hands slid from my hips and cupped my butt, jerking me against his front. Jeez. Was it me or were all demons hornier than a cat in heat?

"Either you have, or you haven't," I growled, shoving his hands off my body and no longer keeping up the pretense of dancing.

The demon tucked his hands in his pockets and grinned a toothy smile. "What's in it for me?"

It was my turn to grin. Leaning ever so slightly toward him, I trailed a finger along his bulging pectoral. "You get to live." I pushed a bit of my holy power into his chest. Okay, the teeny tiny bit I had built back up, so it was more like a zap than a knock you on your ass kind of hit. However, it did make the demon wince, so I counted that as a win but not so much the dark chuckle afterward.

"Ouch, you know, that kind of hurt." He beamed down at me, far too flirty and not acting evil enough. The way I liked my demons.

"Stop that." I scowled, moving out of his grasp.

"Stop what?"

"That." I waved a finger in his direction.

"I don't believe I know what you are referring to." He crossed his arms over his chest, exuding confidence and far too much dominance for my liking.

"You're a demon," I shouted over the music, earning me a few looks. "You're not supposed to be flirting with me."

"Is that what I'm doing?" He grinned grew. "I thought we were negotiating my survival."

I growled and refrained from stomping my foot like a petulant child. "That's not what you're doing." I glared at the speakers. It was too loud. I couldn't think let alone be intimidating if I couldn't even think. "Is there somewhere else we can do this?"

Throwing his head back to laugh, a sound that rolled through me in a not so unpleasant way, the demon offered me his arm. "I thought you'd never ask."

Eyeing the arm like it was a rattle snack ready to bite me at any time, I debated with myself. I did ask to go somewhere more private, but I was starting to think it was a bad idea. Not seeing much of another option, I took his arm and let him lead me through the crowd. Farther back in the building there were curtained off areas with various sounds coming from them. The music wasn't as loud back here, and there was a level of intimacy that I didn't care for.

The demon led us over to an empty booth and released me to allow me to slide into the seat. I started to pull the curtain closed, but I made a sound. He looked over his shoulder and raised a brow. "I thought you wanted privacy?"

I cleared my throat and shifted in my seat. "Not that kind of privacy."

Shrugging a shoulder, the demon left the curtain open and sat in the seat next to me. Scooching closer to me on the bench he threw his arms over the back of the u-shaped booth. "So, what will it be?"

I gaped at him for a moment. "What will what be?"

"You want me to shapeshift into this kid you showed me?" He nodded his head toward the picture still in my hand. "Though, he seems a bit young for an angel. I'd think you'd want something more... well..." He chuckled, brushing his hand through his hair. "This."

I had to admit it took me far longer to figure out what the demon in front of me was talking about before I finally caught on. Trisha and Adara would both be ashamed of me.

"You think I want to have sex with you."

The demon pursed his lips and his eyes locked with mine. For the first time, his grin dropped. "You didn't come here for sex?"

"Uh, no." I shook my head, utterly confused. "Hold on, I thought this was a vampire club? Like vampires kidnapping kids to feed on. That kind of thing."

This time it was the demon that looked confused. "No, it hasn't been a vamp club since the seventies."

"Then what's with the name?"

He shrugged. "Lazy owners."

I huffed. "Fuck. Look. You seem like a nice enough demon, I'd hate to have to leave another body to clean up. Why don't you just get out of this guy and we can both be on our way?"

"I can't do that."

"Why not?"

"Because I'm under contract and besides this guy's soul was gone when I took the body." He waved a hand over his way too delectable form. "If I leave, you still have a dead body on your hands."

Gritting my teeth, I bit out. "Fine. Keep the freaking body. Just tell me, have you seen this boy?"

The demon took the picture I held up again and really looked at it this time. "Yeah, he came in here a while ago. He's in booth eight. But he's already-"

I didn't wait for him to finish, I got up and started for the booth counting them as I went. Ripping open the curtain of what I presumed was booth eight, I found Henry Barnes sucking off a forty-year-old gentleman. The gentleman jumped in his seat, but once his eyes landed on me, they filled with lust. "Oh, Henry. I didn't know you had a surprise for me."

"I didn't," Henry said, stopping what he was doing to look at me. "What do you want?"

I didn't have to ask to know that Henry was like the other guy. Dead as a doornail with a demon inside. His skin was pale like that of a cadaver, his body was far worse for wear than my beefcake hottie. Henry was dead, and a demon was parading around in his body.

185

"I'm here on behalf of the parents of the body you're riding."

"The what?" The older man stared at me and then at Henry.

Henry - or the demon inside of Henry - slid out of the booth. "Excuse me, I'll be right back." We moved a short distance away from the booth before Henry seethed. "What the fuck is wrong with you? Do you want to give away what we are?"

I snorted, crossing my arms over my chest. "Speak for yourself, demon."

"You're not a..."

Just then my handsome guide from before showed up. "Henry, I'm sorry for the intrusion. This lovely angel..." Henry's eyes widened in surprise but not terror. Really what was wrong with demons these days? "... was looking for the body you are currently using."

"Why?"

"The parents are looking for their son of course. They want to know what happened to him." I waved a hand up and down his form. "I can see now that I'll have to go back and tell them you're dead. Now, if you could just get out of his body so they have someone to bury, that would be great."

Henry and the handsome one exchanged a look before Henry spoke, "See, there's a problem with that. While I would love to avoid the violence you are no doubt waiting to unleash upon me, the owner of this body signed his body away to be used here at the club. I can't just give it back."

My nose wrinkled. "In exchange for what? He's dead."

"For a quick and painless death," the handsome one explained. "See, we offer those who are depressed and looking for a way out... well, an out."

"So, you're pretty much assisting in suicide. You know that is illegal in most states and most certainly not okay," I snapped, glaring at the two of them. "And do these people know you are using their bodies for prostitution?"

"Oh, yeah. Of course. It's all in the contract." Henry nodded, starting for the first time to seem a bit green around the gills. Good, you should be afraid, you piece of demon filth.

"And assisted suicide is legal in Washington."

"For terminally ill people, not depressed college kids who should have gone to a doctor instead of a demon who sent him to Hell faster," I shouted, pulling the knife out of my cleavage and pointed it at his jugular. "You give me this body back or so help me God, I'll destroy you too."

Henry held his hands up, trying to seem as defenseless as possible. A large hand clamped down on my hand holding the knife, and the handsome one urged me to lower it.

"Look, we don't want any trouble here. We're only doing our jobs. If you want the kids' body back, fine, but wouldn't the parents be happier knowing their kid is alive and well rather than dead?"

I frowned. He had a point. I hated that.

The handsome one lowered my arm, and I let him. "Then just give Henry the parents' contact information. He'll pop by and give them a heads up about where he's been, etc., etc., so on and so forth. Everyone is happy, and nobody has to die."

"What's he going to tell them? He's been going down on middle-aged men for money?"

I eyeballed the man still waiting in Henry's booth.

"No, of course not." Henry shook his head. "I'll tell them I went on a road trip with friends and just got back. I lost my phone and needed some space. You'll be surprised how often it works. Parents are only happy to see their kid alive."

I tapped my knife against my pant leg and thought for a moment. He wasn't wrong. And I was pretty sure Mrs. Barnes would be happier with a living son than a dead one. I'd hate to lose the money because she was grieving. Fuck. Trisha won't like this.

"Fine. You can keep the body, BUT you have to go make nice with the parents. Make it believable, they're my clients so they'll tell me if something is off." I pointed the knife in his direction, and he gulped and nodded. I told him the Barnes' phone number and address I got off my phone before he wandered back to his booth and his waiting... client.

Sighing heavily, I tucked my knife back into my cleavage. The handsome one was still there watching me. "What?"

"Well, you're off duty, now right? Did you want to...?" He waved a hand toward the booth.

A flush overcame my cheeks, and I cleared my throat. "No. No way." I started to tell him to fuck off and then remembered what Octavia said. "But if you are looking to make some money... I have a job for you."

14

THE FLIGHT BACK TO L.A. was a bit more interesting with the handsome demon guy who I'd learned goes by Todd. Really, Todd for a demon? I was pretty sure it was the body's name and not his, but I wasn't going to bother with the technicalities. I needed the demon for my ritual and who knew what that entailed. He might end up being staked to an altar. Getting attached especially to a demon was not a good idea. It was bad enough Sid was half.

"So, what exactly is it you need me to assist with?" Todd asked as we climbed out of the taxi I'd called to pick us up. I didn't want Trisha asking too many questions especially if she already knew what Octavia wanted the demon for.

"I'm trying to get to Hell, and I was told a demon could help." I tried to be as vague as possible. It wasn't hard since I didn't really know what I needed him for myself. I hoped Octavia would explain everything today.

We started up the driveway of the Phoenix Guild mansion with Todd on my heels. When I walked up the stairs, Todd made a surprised grunt. Turning around, I found him trying to walk up the stairs but unable to get past some kind of force field.

"What is it?" I climbed down the stairs to where he stood. I frowned. I didn't feel anything different.

"I don't know. It's like the house is warded or something." He pushed his hand out, but it bounced right back off the invisible barrier.

Scowling, I turned from him and walked up the steps. "Hold on." Shoving the front door open, I hollered, "Adara! Where are you?"

After a few seconds of quiet, Adara came running out of the office door. She had her gun in one hand and a sword in another.

"What? What is it? Are we under attack? I sensed a demon on the barrier."

"Yeah," I snapped. "My demon. The one Octavia said I needed for this spell? Now can you lift the barrier or what?"

"Oh." Adara's brows furrowed, and she dropped her weapons by her side. "You could have just called."

I threw my hands up. "I didn't know you have a barrier around the place. It doesn't keep angels out."

"Maybe we should fix that huh?" Adara teased, holstering her gun but keeping her sword out. "So, this demon is it secured?"

I arched a brow. "As secure as Todd can be."

"Todd?" Adara gaped. "Your demon's name is Todd."

"Just come to see for yourself." I moved out of the doorway and back down the front steps. Todd stood with his large arms crossed over his chest, an impatient frown on his face.

Adara's footsteps slowed as she took in my demon. I watched her face as her eyes widened and her mouth dropped open. "Wow, Mary. You sure know how to pick 'em."

"Wipe the drool off your chin, Adara. This one's not for you." I waved a hand in front of her face, promptly ignoring the smug expression on Todd's face. "And you, keep those slimy hands and that smooth talking to yourself. In fact, it'd be better for everyone if you just don't talk. Today you are mute." I mimed closing his mouth with my hand. "Now come on, we're wasting daylight here." I gestured at Adara to hurry up.

"Right, sorry." Adara cleared her throat and then closed her eyes. Pressing a fist to her palm, she muttered under her breath and then opened her eyes. "There. You should be able to get through now Mr. Todd the demon." She smiled a bit too brightly at him, making me have the sudden urge to smack her over the head. Did she think with any other than her vagina?

Todd tested the barrier and then when his hand went through, sighed. "Thank you, you are as helpful as you are lovely." He winked at her, and I stepped between them.

"No." I pointed a finger at Adara and then turned to Todd. "What'd I say? Mute. If you want to get out of your contract, you need to do as I say."

"Fine," Todd muttered, his eyes ducking down in mock reverence, but I wasn't fooled.

"Let's get this over with." I climbed back up the stairs not paying Adara and Todd anymore mind as I made my way to the office. Octavia sat with Trisha having a cup of tea. When I entered the room, they both looked up.

"Mary, finally." Trisha jumped up from her seat and run over to me. Wrapping her arms around my waist, I allowed her to hug me for a few moments. "I was so worried when you said you were coming home, and you'd found a demon for the ritual."

I patted her head and smiled softly. "Everything turned out alright."

"I heard." Trisha beamed. "Mrs. Barnes called this morning saying how Henry had shown up at their doorstep and it's all thanks to you. So, where was he?"

I forced a smile. "You wouldn't believe me if I told you."

Thankfully, before Trisha could ask me any more questions Adara and Todd entered

195

the office. Just like Adara, Trisha's mouth dropped open, and she forgot how to function. Really, Todd's host body was not that attractive.

"Who is that?"

I sighed and took one of the empty seats near Octavia. "That's our demon for the night," I told Trisha as I poured myself a cup of tea. To Octavia, I asked, "Will he work? You didn't specify what type of demon."

Octavia's eyes scanned over Todd a bit more thoroughly than needed, and a small smile touched her lips. "Yes, he will do quite nicely."

"Good," I quipped, stirring sugar into my tea. "So, can you tell me what this ritual entails? The full moon is tonight."

Todd and Adara moved further into the room as Octavia shifted in her seat, preparing to explain. "First, I need to know that you have not changed your mind about this." Octavia locked her eyes with me, the intensity in them making me want to squirm.

I forced myself to stay still and lifted my chin. "Yes, of course. Nothing has changed."

"Very well." Octavia sat her cup down. "Then the ritual will start at dark when the moon is at its highest peak. We will need to draw a pentagram on the floor and call upon the five elements. Then there is a bit of mumbo-jumbo on my part." Trisha giggled at her words causing Octavia to smile. "Mary and the demon—"

"Todd," Adara interjected beaming at the demon.

"Mary and Todd will both have an herbal paste placed on them that will open up their spirits." I started to argue that we don't have spirits, but Octavia shot me a warning look like she knew what I was going to say. "Now, this is the hard part." She took a deep breath as if to steel herself for my objections. "You will take the demon's energy into yourself, and that will allow you to break the barrier between the planes."

The room was quiet for a moment before the whole room burst into a panic.

"What the hell do you mean she has to take the demon into her? Like sex?" Trisha wrinkled her nose.

Todd made a disgusted sound, his arms crossing over his chest. "I'm not being absorbed into her. I like this body."

Adara grinned, staring at Todd with admiration in her eyes. "So do I. I have plans for that body. You can't just make him jump ship like that."

"I am so not putting that thing inside of me."

"Would you all calm down?" Octavia tried to shush us, but we wouldn't listen, each of us having our own argument for why this was so not happening. "QUIET!" The room shook around us, and we promptly went silent.

"Now, I understand your concerns," Octavia began, her eyes moving around the room. "But you asked me for a way into Hell, and this is it. No, you don't have to have sex with him. You are taking his essence in like you would do with an exorcism, but instead of destroying it with your own powers, you'll hold it. And you," - she looked to Todd - "if you want out of your contract, you're going to have to give up that body. Don't think I don't know what kind of work you do. This is the only way." Taking a deep breath in, she let it out before picking her teacup back up.

"Now are we going to go through with this or not because my plants need to be watered and my wards need to be reinforced."

Frowning, I crossed my arms over my chest and tapped my foot. I needed to get into Hell, that was true. However, I never expected that need to force me to take something like a demon inside of me. The very thought of it made my skin crawl. Thankfully, Todd didn't seem too thrilled about it either.

"Fine." Todd tucked his hands into his pockets and rocked back and forth on his heels. "If it's the only way to get me out of my contract, I'll do it, but you have to promise to find me a new body after all this."

My lips twisted into an unhappy grimace. "I suppose I can do that. As long as it's someone dead or dying. I won't let you kill someone's soul."

"Deal." He held his hand out to me, and I reluctantly shook it.

"Now, hold on a minute," Trisha interrupted our little exchange. "You don't know what this will do to you," she whispered, kneeling in her chair so she could see me. "You're still recovering from you

199

know what and he might overpower you. Next thing you know you're on the next episode of *Body Snatchers*."

I rolled my eyes and placed a hand on her arm. "It's fine, Trisha. We need this. And if it comes down to it, you and Adara can exorcize him out of me, right?"

Trisha pursed her lips for a moment before giving me a tight nod.

"Good. Now that it's all settled let's get this show on the road." Adara clapped her hands together and then gestured out the door. We'll use the main room for this, it'll be easier to clean off the floor."

"Famous last words," Trisha muttered as we all filed out of the room.

15

THE HOURS LEADING UP to the ritual were brutal. Liking pull teeth without any numbing agent. Trisha spent the time biting down every nail she had to the quick, her eyes drifting from me to Todd every few minutes. She looked like she wanted to say something several times but then stopped at the last second.

Adara didn't seem too worried about it all. Instead of bothering with the logistics, she spent the time flirting with Todd. No doubt trying to get him into bed before he had to shed that body. I couldn't blame her I guess. It was a nice body. Too bad it belonged to someone else.

Octavia, of course, wasn't the calmest of us all. She went about setting the site up with her candles and purification sage. I helped her draw a pentagram on the ground large enough for Todd and me to lay down in. I wasn't sure why it mattered if we were laying down, but I didn't think to argue.

"It's so you don't fall and bust your head open. The ritual is quite overwhelming," Octavia told me out of the blue, looking up from where we had finished closing the circle.

"It can't be much different from taking one into myself. Which by the way, I don't know why I don't just do what I usually do?"

Octavia began to mix up the paste that she would end up smearing all over Todd and me. "This is not the same thing. When you take a demon inside of you, you're only allowing it to visit. This is different. You won't be taking his essence into you and then dispelling it right afterward. You have to accept him. Make him a part of you, or it won't work."

My brows furrowed tightly. I didn't like how she was explaining this. "I'm an angel. I can't make a demon a part of me. We're the total opposites."

202

"Are you really?" She arched a brow at me. "The way I understand it, demons are merely humans or sometimes angels who have lost their way. Who knows? Maybe you can help this Todd find his way back."

"Pfft. I didn't sign up to be a redeemer of demons. I'm trying to save my boyfriend and stop the apocalypse." I jerked my arm out to the side, frustrated at where this conversation was going.

"And you can do all that with this demon." She sighed and rubbed the extra powder she had on her hands onto her skirt. "But it will require you to open yourself up to him. If you destroy him before you can pass through to the other side, then the portal will rip you to pieces."

"Hold up, what did you just say?" Trisha interjected into our conversation, looking even more worried than before. Trisha outcry drew the attention of Adara and Todd who stopped talking and moved closer to the circle.

Octavia didn't even seem bothered by all the attention and simply continued her preparations. "The portal I can create will allowing allow someone of demon nature through, hence the reason you have to take the demon into yourself. Since your gentleman friend is already half-demon he won't have an issue getting back, but if you try to exorcize Todd before you come back, you'll be stuck there or worse..."

The clear warning in her voice did not get overlooked by Trisha or Adara. I could tell Trisha was waiting to blow up and convince me not to do the whole thing. Adara knew better than to try to convince me to do anything. Besides, she was already planning her and Todd's wedding as we spoke. Or at least, how to get him out of his pants and into hers.

"Todd?" I arched a brow because if anyone had a say in this, then it was him. "How do you feel about this whole situation?"

Todd scratched the back of his head. "Look, while the situation isn't ideal, it sure beats being stuck back in Hell or going down on some old guy for the chance of getting him to sell his soul over."

Trisha gaped at him in a mixture of disgust and curiosity. She watches way too many of those cartoons. I swear they have rotted her brain.

"Alright." I stood to my feet, adjusting my gun holster as I stood. "If you're good with it, then I am. But after this, you're out of here, alright? Maybe Sid can give you a job at the bar or something?"

Octavia snorted in amusement but didn't comment. Instead, she climbed to her feet using her cane to help her, she ushered Todd and me closer to her. "Now, the moon has just about reached its peak. Are you ready?"

Nodding, I knelt before her like she had instructed before. Todd took his place next to me and tried to hold my hand. I gave him an incredulous glare, pulling my hand back to myself. I might have to take this guy into myself, but I wasn't playing touchy feely.

Dipping her fingers into the bowl, she had finished mixing she rubbed the stinky paste across my forehead and then Todd's. It tingled against my skin, and I had the itching urge to rub it off. However, I somehow refrained from giving in to my urge and gritted my teeth forcing myself to do what had to be done.

"Now, take your place in the center of the circle." She pressed her hands together and gestured toward the center.

Todd and I laid down in the middle of the circle, our hands barely touching each other. I started to move my hand away, but Octavia spoke up. "You might as well get used to it he's about to be a whole lot closer than that."

Trisha giggled on the sideline and I shot her a glare. She cut her laughter off, feigning zipping her lips. Adara finally started to look worried, her brows drawn in tight.

"It'll be fine," I reassured her. She gave me a tight smile, but it didn't make her look any less worried.

"Now, Adara has assured me we won't be interrupted by any of her colleagues." Octavia exchanged a look with Adara looking for confirmation.

Adara inclined her head. "The top part is mostly a front, in any case, most of them are down in the lower levels. I have also instructed everyone to stay clear of this area for twenty-four hours."

So, that's why we hadn't had any more interruptions from her less than happy underlings. Oh, well. I was sure they'd find out eventually and have all kinds of things to complain about to Adara. Her problem, not mine.

"So, what do we do now?" Todd asked, leaning his head up.

"Simply lay there and try to relax. Don't fight it," Octavia instructed with no hint of reassurance. I heaved a deep breath and sighed. The timer Adara had set on her phone began to go off announcing it was time to start the ritual.

My heart began to pound in my chest as Octavia lit a few candles next to her, muttering some words in Latin. Something about cleansing the space and asking for protection against outside forces. She then used the same mixture she put on Todd and me on herself, changing more words. The air around us thickened, and the hairs on my arms stood on end. I turned my head toward Todd to see if he was feeling the same thing I was and found him a bit worse for wear.

His face paled, and his chest jerked up and down as if something was pulling on him from the inside. Todd's mouth opened in a silent scream. A low growling began from somewhere inside his throat, and it made Octavia curse.

"Don't fight it, Todd. You'll only make it worse."

Not wanting to lose the only chance we had to get into Hell, I grabbed Todd's hand. "It's alright. I'm here. Think of it like when you are going into a body but in reverse. Let yourself pour out of this one. Relax. Breathe."

"Easy for you to say," Todd gasped, his voice raspy and more demonic than before. "You're not getting your insides torn apart."

I chuckled. "Yeah, well, it's about to get very crowded in here, so we'll call it a tradeoff." I squeezed his hand in mine. "Relax."

Todd closed his eyes, and his shoulders sagged. With his next exhale of breath, a thick cloud of smoke poured out of his mouth and hovered in the air. I watched it with wide eyes and a feeling of trepidation. When the smoke moved from him and over to me, I swallowed thickly and opened my mouth, preparing myself for the onslaught of his essence. Without warning, it charged at me, shoving its way down my throat and into my very being. My body seized up and tried to reject Todd.

"Relax, Mary," Trisha murmured from the sidelines.

Not wanting to worry her, I closed my eyes and breathed in the rest of the smoke allowing it to fill me up to the brink. Clipping my mouth shut, I fought the instincts telling me to purify myself to purge my aura of the black spots that had appeared. After a few minutes of struggling, Todd's essence settled within me.

Why can't I see?

Todd's voice - the demon's voice - filled my head. He no longer sounded like the smooth talker from before, but it didn't mean his voice was any less appealing. The parts of him inside of me swirled around in my chest touching places of me that I had never imagined would be touched. It was provocative in a way. Perverse.

I'd hardly say that.

"Can you hear all my thoughts?" Blinking my eyes open, I sat up.

Ah, that's better. So, this is what an angel sees? Interesting.

I snorted. "Hardly."

"Mary?" Adara knelt beside me, caution in her every movement. "Are you alright?"

I turned to her, shifting from the ground to my knees. "I feel a bit strange, but for the most part I feel alright." I rolled my shoulders and took inventory of my body, then nodded. "Everything is the same, except I can feel him... here." I touched my chest. "And hear him in my head."

"Weird." Trisha crept closer as if I were an animal on display. She waved her hand in front of my face. "Can he see that?"

Yes.

"Yes, now stop." I grabbed her hand and pushed it back to her. "We don't have time for another game of twenty questions."

Trisha pouted but relented.

"Are you ready to pass through the portal?" Octavia asked us with a cock of her eyebrow.

"What do you say, Todd? Is your name really Todd?"

Laughter filled my head, and a strange tingle moved down my arm. *No, but you can continue to call me that human name... for now.*

"Fine. Have your secrets. Are you ready or not?" I planted my hands on my hips waiting for him to make up his mind.

Of course, my angel. Whatever you wish.

Snorting, I twisted around to where Octavia waited. "We're ready."

Inclining her head, Octavia reached into her pouch she had tied to her hip and threw it in the air. A word spoken too low for me to catch and the powder began to swirl and glow before becoming larger. Eventually, it expanded so far that it was big enough for a person to walk through.

Now that doesn't look safe.

"Stop your bitching," I grumbled under my breath. "At least you are going home."

It's called Hell for a reason. Even the residents want to get out. Todd's laughter trailed off as I stepped through the portal and back into Hell.

16

FOR A MOMENT, I thought Octavia had been wrong. I'd only been through two portals in my life. The first one when I had been taken by the demons, and I hadn't thought much about how that went about or what the sensation of the transition between the planes had been like. I was too busy fighting to get away.

The second time had been when I had finally gotten away from the demons. I also hadn't paid much mind to the portal, only the act of getting out.

Now, though. Now I only had more than enough time to notice the portal. It pulled at my skin as if searching me out, trying to decipher what I was and if it would allow me in.

Don't worry, angel. It'll let us through.

I ignored Todd's voice inside my head and focused on trying to make myself seem more like a demon. If I could pull my angelic powers deeper inside myself, I would have, but as it was, I didn't have much to hide. Two months was not enough time to recover to my full strength. I was already taking a huge risk going to Hell by myself, even worse with a demon inside of me who might change sides at any moment.

I am offended you would think that way.

I rolled my eyes and finally stepped out of the portal with a sigh. Thankfully, the surrounding walls looked familiar. I'd come back to the same place I'd gone in my spirit quest. Not wanting to risk being heard, I kept my words in my head. *You're a demon. You only think about saving yourself.*

A dark chuckle filled my mind and rolled through my body. I forced myself to ignore the tingle of pleasure it gave. *Not all demons are alike, just like not all angels are so pure and innocent. There is a reason Hell became what it is.*

He didn't have to clarify his words. I knew what he was talking about. Lucifer had been the purest and best of us, but he had fallen. Turned his once beautiful essence into a gaping black pit of despair which he then decided to fill with every soul on Heaven and Earth.

Not if I could help it.

I stared down at the cell that I had once been in before, the place that still haunted my nightmares. The rock they had strapped me down to as they chopped at my wings was stained brown from my blood. It was hard to look away from now that I was there in physical form. I could feel the edges of my mind darkening on me. The pain of what happened to me overtaking my mind.

Mary. Mary. Muriel, snap out of it. We don't have time for this.

Todd screaming in my head finally made me blink. I scanned around me, and the darkness receded. This room couldn't hurt me anymore. I was fine. I could make it through this... for Sid.

Great for Sid the half demon. Not for yourself or, you know, the demon you are hijacking.

Oh, shut it.

I walked toward the door to my cell, ignoring the demon in my head having a one-sided conversation. I had a feeling this was going to get old fast.

All the better reason to get in there, get your knife, your guy, and get out.

It's Michael's blade, not a knife.

If Todd could roll his eyes, I bet he was doing it right now but, in any case, he was silent. At least for now.

Poking my head out of the door, I searched the hallway. It was empty and quiet. Not something I was going to complain about. I tried to remember which way I had gone last time and inched my way out of the cell. The door closed with a loud creak that made me wince.

Nice one.

Fuck off.

When I got to the fork, I turned right instead of left. Last time, Sid had been hiding from the demons searching from him in the left hallway, meaning he had come from the right. There was a line of doors like the one to my torture chamber that way, but they weren't as quiet as mine had been.

Screams came from one on the left. To the right, someone moaned as if in pain. More than likely they were. I tried not to think about it too much as I moved down the hallway. I was surprised I hadn't run into any demons yet but couldn't find a good enough reason to complain about it.

Do you even know where you're going?

Quiet, I'm trying to listen.

There was one door in the hallway that was different from the rest of them. Not only was the door locked but there was a large beam running across it as if the lock wasn't enough to keep them inside.

This has to be it.

Well, what are you waiting for an invitation?

My lips twisted in a scowl but didn't argue. I grabbed the handle of the beam and pushed with all my might. However, it didn't budge. *A little help here, please.*

216

Oh, the big and mighty angel is asking for my help? Little ole me?

"You know, I liked you better when you were only trying to get in my pants," I grunted as I shoved at the beam some more. A chuckle sounded in my head, but then a boost of strength caused the beam to move so suddenly that I almost fell on my face.

Real smooth.

"Fuck off," I growled and then pulled back the lock on the door. I jerked the door to the cell open faster than I should have. If I had been smart, I'd have waited to see what was in there first before going in guns blazing. I blame the demon in my head though for my rashness. Fortunately, I didn't have anything to worry about.

Inside the room, tied to the bed was Sid. They had stripped him down to nothing and left him there. There wasn't even a sheet to cover his private parts or keep him warm. Not that he needed it in Hell, it was this side of too toasty.

A delectable piece of meat, that one is.

I didn't question the demon's preference in genders or if only he were only saying things to make me uncomfortable. I was used to it though. Trisha and Sid had already desensitized me to everything sex-related. There couldn't be much more to shock me.

A husky laughter filled me. *Oh, Mary. So young. So pure.*

Rolling my eyes at him, I slowly approached the bed. Sid's eyes were closed like was sleeping. His chest rising and falling in a rhythmic pattern. I stood at the side of the bed just watching him for a moment before reaching a hand out.

Suddenly, Sid's eyes popped open and his what I thought was tied up hands grabbed mine. The next things I knew I was on my back and Sid's hands were around my throat. I fought against him. I grabbed at his hands and tried to buck him off me.

"Sid, stop. It's me. Mary."

"No, you're not. Stop pretending like you're her. I won't feed. You can't make me." Sid's manic expression filled me with fear. What had they been doing to him? Suddenly, the whole set-up made sense. The bed. The lack of clothing. Of course, his dad didn't think much about raping his own son, forcing him to feed so he won't die.

There are worse things. Todd's voice in my head did nothing for the situation even though I wanted to argue with him. There were worse things yes but for someone like Sid. Someone who hated what he was and what he had to do to survive being forced to feed to have sex was worse than death.

Unfortunately, even though I agreed with Sid, I couldn't let him kill me before we got out of here. I let go of his hands and went for my gun. Flicking the safety, I pointed it at his head. The sound of the bullet turning in the barrel seemed to knock something loose in Sid's mind. His hands around my throat loosened, and his eyes widened.

"Mary?"

"Yeah," I coughed, but never taking my eyes or my gun off him. "It's me. No illusion. No trick. I came to Hell to save you." Sid stared at me harder as if he couldn't comprehend what I was saying. I shifted my hip and offered him a smile. "Either get off me or fuck me because being this close to you naked is kind of torture."

A hint of a smile finally crept up Sid's lips. Then those lips were on mine. I lowered the gun and let him kiss me. The heat of his mouth engulfed mine, and I allowed myself to enjoy his embrace for a moment.

Not to break up this love fest, but we're still in Hell. I don't know about you, but I don't want to be caught with my pants down.

Sadly, he was right. I broke the kiss with a hand to Sid's chest. "We have to go. No one knows I'm here yet, but they will soon if we don't leave."

Sid moved off me with great reluctance. Standing in the room completely nude, Sid placed his hands on his hips drawing my attention down low. Turning my head away, I flushed. While I appreciated his body, we needed to find him some clothes.

"How did you even get here? I thought there were no portals."

Climbing off the bed, I shook my head. "Well talk about it later. Right now, we need to find Michael's blade and leave before..."

The door to the cell busted open and in poured three backward legged demons. I didn't hesitate, I pointed my already upholstered gun at them and fired three shots. They dropped like bugs, but I didn't let myself relax. Running over to the only demon I had seen with some scrap of

220

clothing on, I disrobed him and tossed them toward Sid. "Get dressed. Someone will have heard that. We can't stay here."

Sid dressed quickly, and we made for the door. The hallway was empty for now, but I didn't expect it to stay that way long. I could hear rumblings of feet in the distance. "Come on, this way." I started to go back the way we came, but Sid stopped me.

"The blade."

While I wanted to get the blade, I also knew what happened last time Sid went for it. The moment that door opened Asmodeus would know. The demons were already coming for us, and they would know exactly where to go too.

Leave it. You have your man.

Can't. Want to. But can't. I couldn't leave that dagger with them. They would simply find another way to lash out at me to get me to do what they wanted. Or worse, take someone else I loved.

"Okay, you go toward the vault." I pointed down the hallway. "I'll back you up." Holding my gun up, I ushered him toward the vault while keeping my eyes peeled for demons.

The moment Sid hit the vault, six demons came for us.

"There! Take them." The leader of them hissed and snapped.

"Hurry up, Sid," I shouted over my shoulder pointing my gun at them. I got four shots off before they got to us. The last two attacked me as one.

Ducking at the clawed fist coming at my face, I spun around slinging my leg out to kick its leg out from under it. When it landed, I shot it in the head. The last demon grabbed me by the back of the hair and dragged me to them. Straddling me, it tried to cut at my throat with its massive claws. I grabbed its wrists and struggled against it, trying to roll us so that I was on top. When I finally managed to turn it around, I shouted at Sid. "A bit faster if you please."

"Almost got it," Sid called back.

The demon had my gun hand, so I pulled the knife I still had in my cleavage out. I stabbed the demon in the neck and stood. Grinning, I turned around to find Asmodeus holding Sid by the back of the shirt, Michael's blade in his hand.

"Looking for this?"

17

I STARED AT ASMODEUS for a moment, assessing my choices. He had Sid and Michael's blade. I needed to end this now before any more demons came barreling through that hallway.

"What do you want?"

Asmodeus smiled that beautiful but cruel smile of his. "It's not a question of what I want but what you want."

I sniffed. "I want Sid and Michael's blade. If that comes with your head on a plate, I'd take that too."

"Always making jokes." Asmodeus chuckled, shaking his head. "I think we both know what you really want."

Your wings.

I pushed the thought away. I knew that hoping to get my wings, Sid, and Michael's blade was a long shot. The way things were now I would once again have to leave them behind but Asmodeus didn't need to know that.

"Where are they?" I shifted my stance.

"They're safe. Give me what I want, and you can have everything you want. My son, your wings." He smirked. "All you have to do is open one little portal for us."

"And you know the answer is no. It will always be no." I lifted my gun up, pointing it at Asmodeus's head.

Asmodeus jerked Sid in front of him. "Now, now. Let's play nice. I need my son alive, but I won't sacrifice myself for him."

Father of the Year, this one.

I ignored Todd's taunting and focused on Asmodeus. I couldn't shoot him when he was hiding behind Sid. There was no choice. I couldn't do what Asmodeus wanted me to do especially since I knew that Lucifer was behind all of this. So, either I do what he wanted or leave without either of the things I came for, making this all for nothing.

However, I could wound him. Maybe give us enough time to get Michael's dagger and Sid and get the hell out of there.

You're not seriously thinking about...

It's my only choice.

Without another thought, I locked eyes with Sid and shifted my aim. The shot rang out and filled the vault. Sid flinched but didn't scream like I knew he wouldn't. However, his father, who was all demon, cried out like a baby as the holy bullet ripped through his shoulder. Asmodeus let go of Sid to clutch his wound, giving Sid the opening to grab Michael's blade from him. He kicked Asmodeus in the stomach, sending him to the floor.

"Come on!" I grabbed Sid's arm and dragged him out of there. Racing down the hallway, I didn't pause when the demons poured in at the other side. I shot at them as we kept moving, running for the portal. Demons were nipping on both of our heels, and I was out of bullets. We weren't going to make it, not like this, and we couldn't let those demons get through.

I could help if you just say please.

"If you could help, why didn't you say that earlier?" I snarled at him.

"Who are you talking to?" Sid stared at me over his shoulder.

I shook my head. "Never mind." *What do you want me to do, beg?*

A please would be nice.

Fine. Please.

There's a good angel. I didn't have a chance to ask him what he was going to do before I lost control of my body. Stopping my tracks, I turned toward the oncoming demons. A swell of energy built up inside of me, and then like a trigger, it burst forth, turning all the demons in the hallway to black smoke and dust.

"Wow, when did you learn to do that?" Sid asked, his eyes wide with terror and awe.

I regained control of my body and heaved in a big breath. *What the hell was that?*

226

You wanted help.

Waving him off, I told Sid, "A lot has changed, but we can talk about it later." Not allowing him to ask me anything else, I turned back toward the portal. "Let's get out of here."

Before we could get all the way to the portal, there was a rumbling.

"Crap, we have to hurry." Sid and I ran for the portal neither of us looking back to see what was coming after us. We threw ourselves through the portal and landed with a hard thud on the floor of the Phoenix Guild.

"Mary!" Trisha rushed to my side. She rolled me over, searching me for injuries.

"Octavia, close the portal now," Adara shouted, her gun going off, but she was shooting at nothing. No one was going to follow us. Todd had made sure of that.

You're welcome.

"I'm fine. Stop." I pushed her hands away from me and glanced over at Sid. "Get something to stop the bleeding before you bleed out on this nice marble floor."

"Such a romantic, this one." Sid waved a hand but didn't get up either. It seemed both of us were too relieved to do anything else. Adara moved to his side and started to work on Sid.

I'm good too. Thanks for asking, Todd's voice filled my head, and I sighed.

Now that's a shame.

"Mary!" Trisha tugged on my arm. I rolled my head over to look at her. "Your phone's going off like crazy."

Groaning, I inched up to a seated position and grabbed my phone. Thompson. "Please tell me you can handle whatever you're calling for?"

Thompson chuckled on the other line. "Actually, I called to let you know I found our demon. We have him. I wanted to know what you think we should do with him."

Sighing, I rubbed a hand over my face. "You have any holy bullets left?"

"I'm not going to kill him. He hasn't killed anyone yet in this body plus... what would I tell the others?" Thompson lowered his voice like he was trying not to be heard.

"Then you'll have to lock him up and exorcize him."

What about me?

I rolled my eyes at Todd's whining. *You can leave at any time.*

"Can't you come do it?"

Yeah, angel. Can't you?

Just leave already. I scowled.

No, I don't think so. I like it here.

Growling to myself at the annoying pest, I almost forgot the Sergeant was on the phone. "Sure, I'll come to do that," I grunted and laughed at my inability to move. "Just as soon as I figure out how to work my legs again."

18

AN ITCHING IN MY brain woke me. A nagging sort of feeling that wouldn't leave me alone.

I rolled over and stared at Sid. In the moonlight coming in through the window, I could barely make out his sleeping face. Peaceful. That's how he looked. If I didn't know for myself, I'd have said he hadn't spent the last few months in Hell.

When I had left Hell, I wasn't myself anymore. I couldn't sleep. Nightmares plagued my head. I couldn't sleep for weeks. Even now every once in a while, I would dream about my time in Hell. I would wake up in a sweat, my heart pounding, and my head spinning.

Not like tonight though. It wasn't nightmares that kept me awake.

Muriel.

Clenching my teeth, I turned away from Sid's sleeping form. My feet landed on the ice-cold floor as I slipped out of bed. I dragged my t-shirt over my head and pulled my jeans and boots on before quietly moving toward the door.

Muriel. You can't ignore me.

Closing the door behind me, I grabbed my spare gun from Trisha's desk and walked out of the apartment. My shoes banged on the stairs as I headed downstairs. Even though it was late, Lou's was still open, one of the only Chinese places that were open until three a.m. or later, depending on how busy they were. While I was tempted to feed my suddenly growling stomach, I bypassed Lou's and headed into the dark empty store below my office.

The bell above the door chimed. My eyes flicked to the top of the door and without much thought to it, I pulled the bell out of the wall and dropped it on the nearest counter. I winced as it echoed in the room. Moving through the shop, I found the light switch behind Madame Serena's counter.

"Alright, you soul-sucking parasite," I growled into the room though it was clear nobody in the room would answer back.

A chilling laugh filled my head. *Come now, Muriel. It's not all bad. You got what you wanted. Now it's time to give me what I want.*

"And what's that?" I shouted glaring at the unseen demon inside of me. I could feel him moving around like a cancer, creeping into every crevice of my being. If I could I would have cut him out but be it as it may I invited in, it would be a bit harder to get him out.

The laughter started again. This time sending a chill through my body. *What every demon wants?*

"Eternal torment?"

Oh, Muriel. How you love to tease. We're going to have fun, you and me.

"We're not going to have anything," I snapped. Pulling my gun from my holster, I put the barrel of it to my head. "Now, you're going to get out of my body, or I'm going to end this one way or another."

You wouldn't dare, the demon hissed in my mind.

I could feel his teeth biting at me from the inside. I gripped the butt of my gun tighter. I caught the reflection of my face in the glass of the counter. It was one of madness, fury, and above all else determination.

You'd really do it? Destroy us both to get me out?

I didn't have a chance to answer, the door to the shop opened, and Sid walked in. Jeans hanging low, he wore his buttoned-up shirt undone. I quickly lowered my gun as his head turned toward me. Something stirred in me even now at the sight of him. Something that had the demon inside of my head laughing, forgetting that I had just been moments away from ending us both.

"Sidney," I croaked, hiding the gun beneath the counter. "What are you doing in here? You should be resting."

Sid's lips curled up into a grin that made my pulse race for more than fear of being caught. "I could say the same thing about you." He slowly approached the counter, and

233

I shoved the gun into the lower shelf. "It's not every day someone goes into Hell, faces the Devil himself, and live to tell about it."

I let out a nervous chuckle. "Well, what can I say? I have balls of steel."

"That I can believe." Sid came around the counter, his hands sliding onto my hips. His lips dipped down and caught my mouth in a searing kiss. Pulling back, he murmured, "I'll show you mine if you show me yours?"

Grinning despite myself, I tapped his chest the warm skin stretched over his muscle almost enough to tempt me away from the thing inside of me. Almost.

"I have a few things I need to finish down here. How 'bout you head back upstairs, take off all your clothes, and I'll come up in a few minutes?" I arched a brow at him as my fingers slid down his chest to trail along the hair that disappeared into his pants.

Sid smirked, his hands cupping my butt. He pressed me against his lower half, the evidence of his arousal rubbing against me. "Isn't disrobing me something you'd rather do?"

Oh, I like him. Not afraid to be on bottom. Then again, he is a half breed.

I swallowed hard, my own arousal coming to life. The searing laughter in my mind was like a bucket of cold water on my libido. "Maybe next time. I'd rather know you are up there, naked, agonizingly waiting for me to come..." He chuckled knowingly. "Relieve you of your..." I trailed my fingertips along the bulge in his jeans. "... desire."

Kinky.

Shut up. I snapped at the demon in my head. I don't need your commentary.

Laughing darkly, Sid ducked down and nipped my lower lip. "How utterly demonic of you. Maybe something or someone in Hell rubbed off on you."

I tensed up at his words.

"I'm only joking, Mary. Geez." Sid cupped my chin in his hand and pressed a chastise kiss to my nose. When I didn't answer him, he sighed. "Very well, I'll do as you ask but don't keep me waiting too long, or I will have to take matters into my own hands." He wagged his eyebrows at me, and I offered him a reassuring smile.

"I won't be long."

I watched Sid as maneuvered through the shop, pausing at the door to give me a salacious wink before closing the door behind him. My shoulders sagged, and I let out a long breath.

Now, who knew an angel of God would love to get so dirty?

"Shut up," I growled, grabbing my gun from beneath the counter. "I can still end this right now."

And leave the attractive Sidney waiting? Possibly heartbroken? That does not sound like something an angel of God would do. The haughty laugh in my head made me wince.

Scowling, I holstered my gun and flipped off the light. "You still haven't told me what you want. How do I get you out of my head? I am already having a hard enough keeping my form from becoming more human every day the last thing I need is a demon accelerating the process."

Ah, well that is something I can help with. You only have to give up...

"My soul?" I smirked. "Good luck with that one. You and I both know neither of us has a soul. When we're gone, we" - I sucked air in between my teeth - "cease to exist."

236

I don't want your soul. Just a bit of control. You give a little... I get...

"Nothing," I snapped, crossing the dark shop's floor. "You get nothing. I'm not giving you anything but a hot bout of holy water. See how you like it."

Bring it on, love. If I burn, you burn.

Growling as I locked the shop door. "Screw you."

Now, I'll leave that to the delicious demon prince. How will it feel exactly? The demon's voice taunted me. I gritted my teeth and pounded up the stairs. *I haven't been in a body for a while, so I'm quite looking forward to feeling through you. I can be quite distracting when I want to be.*

I paused before the door and glared at the door like I could destroy it with my mind. "Why don't you go back to Hell where you belong?"

Oh, Mary, Mary. You are missing the best part of this whole arrangement. I needed a body, and now I have one. With me inside of you, the angels and demons won't be able to find you. I'm already doing you a favor. Now, why don't you do me one and shag that delightful man?

The reminder that those in Heaven and Hell were looking for me ground my nerves. I was already pressing my luck staying where I was at, having the demon inside of me cloaking me from them was pure luck, and I didn't want to press it.

"Fine. You can stay, for now." I sighed and ran a hand through my hair. "But if we're going to work together what do I call you because I know Todd isn't your name, and it's plain ridiculous." For once, the demon didn't answer me. Shaking my head at even bothering with the demon, I turned the doorknob.

When I opened the front door, Sid called out, "Mary?"

"Yeah, it's me." I hung up my gun holster and kicked off my boots. Forcing myself not to think of the demon writhing around inside of me, I pulled my shirt over my head and unbuttoned my pants. I walked into my room, and my eyes zeroed in on the bed.

Sid had done exactly what I had told him. His clothes lay in a pile on the floor and he in all his scrumptious maleness was spread out on my bed one knee up and a wicked grin on his lips. Licking my lips, my eyes hooded in desire, I crawled onto the edge of the bed.

238

As Sid pulled me into his embrace, that gravelly voice finally answered.

Oh, Muriel. Mary. You, my lovely little broken angel. You can call me Zee.

Thank You for Reading!

Want to find out what happens to Mary Wiles next?

Follow me to be the first to find out!

Don't want to interact but want to be on the up and up?

Follow me on Social Media

Facebook.com/erinrbedford

@erin_bedford

Want to be the first to know about my new releases?

Erinbedford.com/newsletter